"INCREDIBLE. Poignant and lyrical and beautiful, it's my favorite of Kiran's books so far and that is saying something. Tom's stunning artwork just brings it to a whole other level."
Cat Doyle

"Truly extraordinary ... it will redefine what a children's book can look like, in a way that adults will ooh and ahh over, and children will love because the story is wonderful and the art is amazing. It is the kind of book that you will want to have on your shelves and treasure. I can't wait for the world to fall in love with *Julia and the Shark*!"
Katherine Webber Tsang

Praise for
KIRAN MILLWOOD HARGRAVE:

"Hargrave has a real and rare talent for combining poetic prose with compelling, page-turning storytelling."
Guardian

Kiran Millwood Hargrave

Julia and the Shark

with Tom de Freston

union square kids

NEW YORK

**union
square
kids**

NEW YORK

UNION SQUARE KIDS and the distinctive Union Square Kids
logo are trademarks of Union Square & Co., LLC.

Union Square & Co., LLC, is a subsidiary of Sterling Publishing Co., Inc.

Text © 2021 Kiran Millwood Hargrave
Interior illustrations © 2021 Tom de Freston
Cover illustrations © 2021, 2023 Tom de Freston

This edition first published in 2023 by Union Square & Co., LLC.
First published in Great Britain by Hodder & Stoughton Limited in 2021.

ISBN 978-1-4549-4868-1 (hardcover)
ISBN 978-1-4549-4869-8 (paperback)
ISBN 978-1-4549-4870-4 (e-book)

Library of Congress Control Number: 2022946786

For information about custom editions, special sales, and premium purchases,
please contact specialsales@unionsquareandco.com.

Printed in China

Lot #:
2 4 6 8 10 9 7 5 3 1

12/22

unionsquareandco.com

Cover design by Marcie Lawrence
Interior design by Alison Padley

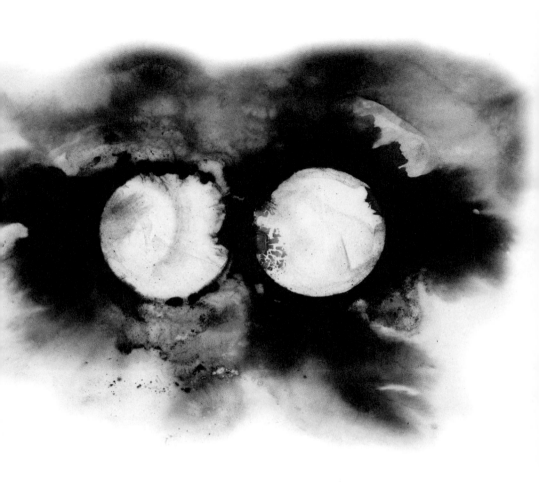

for Rosemary & Lavender,
who made possible all that comes after

One

There are more secrets in the ocean than in the sky. Mum told me when the water is still and the stars prick its surface, some of the sky's secrets fall into the sea and add to its mysteries. When we lived in the lighthouse, I hauled my long-handled crab net over the balcony railing and tried to catch them, but I never did.

Other nights, when storms turned everything upside down and hurled water and sky at each other, the spray from the waves reached the beam. It came through the grates at the high windows to scatter across the floor of Dad's office. I listened to the puddles in the morning, but I never heard anything. No messages fallen from the clouds. Perhaps the secrets drowned in the night, like a fish in air.

My name is Julia. This is the story of the summer I lost my mum and found a shark older than trees. Don't worry though, that doesn't spoil the ending.

I'm named after my grandmother, who I never met, and also after a computer program that my dad likes. I am ten years and two hundred and three days old. I had to ask my dad to work that out for me, because numbers are not my favorite. Words are. You can make numbers into words, but you can't make words into numbers, and so words must be more powerful, mustn't they?

Dad disagrees. He works all in numbers. That's why we ended up at that old lighthouse in Shetland. He went to program it, to make it work automatically. A lighthouse keeper used to live there, and the flame was made of gas and sparks, not a one-thousand watt tungsten light bulb. Gas and sparks, like stars.

It's closer to Norway than England, there. Closer to Norway than Edinburgh, even. To find Shetland on a map, you start at our home in Hayle in Cornwall and you move your finger diagonally up, up and to the right, until you find islands scattered out like ink splatter. That's Orkney. You go even further and there's another scatter. Shetland. It's an archipelago, which means a group of islands, and we went to one called Unst.

Unst, Shetland, Scotland.

I like how people there say it like it's got a whole other bunch of letters in it. Sco-awt-lund. That's another thing about words: there's space in them. They change according to whose mouth they're coming out of. Sometimes they change so much in mine they become something else entirely, but Dad says these are called lies.

There's no room for that with numbers. Even the "language" of numbers, which my dad works with, is called "binary code." If you look up "binary" in the *Oxford English Dictionary* it says:

(adj.) Relating to, composed of, or involving two things.

Two things. Right and wrong. True and false. Where's the space in that?

Mum works with numbers too, but words are her favorite. She's a scientist, which means you need to like both. Numbers help you keep track of things, but only words can help you explain them.

In Cornwall she studied algae, a special kind that cleans the water of any bad chemicals and perhaps one day even breaks up some kinds of plastic. You've probably seen the footage of turtles with plastic up their noses. I did once and it's still there in my head. I wish I could forget it, but perhaps it's fair I can't. Closing your eyes doesn't make things like that go away.

When Dad got offered this job in Shetland it was Mum who suggested us all moving there for the summer. Because while her algae work was important and good for the turtles, moving to Unst meant she would be closer to what she really wanted to study: the biggest things that lived in the coldest seas.

She studied whales at university, and wrote a very long essay about a whale that goes around the world alone because it sings at a different frequency than other whales. It can hear them, but they can't hear it. I understand a little how that whale feels. Ever since Mum got ill, I feel like I've been screaming inside. Yet her favorite animal in all the world wasn't a whale, but a shark. A Greenland shark. And because it was hers, that summer it became mine too.

I like how words are gentler than numbers. I could make everything go back to how it used to be, if I didn't care about this being a true story. If I had to tell you in numbers about my mum, I would have to tell you the most important numbers about her now are 93875400, which is what's on her hospital bracelet. But 93875400 doesn't tell you anything about Mum. Only words can do that. And even they fail me sometimes.

I'm getting tangled. That's the problem with words, and it's the same as the best thing about them. They can mean so many things, and each word has so many branches, so many roots; if you're not sure of the route you can get lost like Little Red Riding Hood in the wood. So I have to go back a bit. I have to remember where I'm trying to get to. And where I'm trying to get to, is Mum.

Reaching Shetland took four days. That's longer than it takes to fly to Australia, which is the other side of the world, and back again. Twice. I didn't think it was possible for anything to take that long now that we have airplanes and bullet trains, but we had to travel there by car because we have books that are too heavy to take on planes, and a cat called Noodle who is too loud to take on trains.

She's called Noodle because she was so tiny when she was a kitten she fit into the empty instant noodle pots Dad ate for lunch. My mum washed them and kept them to plant tomato seeds in because she hated throwing away plastic. You've probably heard of pirates having ship's cats and that is what Noodle is. Mum used to take her out to the algae farms and she'd sit at the front of the boat and hiss at the sea.

There was no question of leaving Noodle behind in Cornwall, so we bought her a special crate to travel in. It was made for dogs and took up nearly all the back seats, so I was squashed to one side with the tomato pots by my feet. Dad set up the crate so that it had levels for her to climb in, and a litter tray in its own little compartment so she would have privacy when she needed it.

"I hope she doesn't poo," said Mum. "It stinks when she poos."

"It stinks when anyone poos," said Dad fairly.

I'm sorry that the first time you're hearing my parents' voices they're talking about poo.

Noodle was too busy meowing very loudly to use the litter tray much. This is a superpower cats have: they can hold their wee a really long time. They are unlike humans in this, and other ways. We stopped loads for toilet breaks and for Mum and Dad to swap driving. They put an audiobook on. It was called *The Crowstarver* by Dick King-Smith and it was very sad and soon we were all crying.

I traced our progress on the road map my parents didn't use anymore because they have a GPS. Maps are more interesting than screens, I think. They show you the whole picture and make roads look like veins or rivers.

We spent the first night in the West Midlands, at a bed-and-breakfast run by a fussy couple who allowed dogs but not cats. It was too late to find anywhere else, so Dad stayed with Noodle in the car while I slept with Mum in the big bed. It had a mattress made of water, which apparently was popular in the olden days.

"It's like sleeping in the belly of a whale," said Mum, shifting around. "All these gurgles and grunts."

"You think?"

"I know. I've heard inside a whale. One swallowed a transmitter we were using to capture them singing. It was louder than the sea in there." Her breathing went all calm like it always did when she talked about the sea.

"Are you excited for the whales in Shetland?"

"Yes." I could hear the smile in her voice. "There are so many kinds. *Balaenoptera musculus. Physeter macrocephalus, Monodon monoceros, Delphinapterus leucas.*"

"Blue whales, sperm whales, narwhals, and belugas," I reeled off, translating her Latin words into ones I could actually pronounce. "It sounds made for you."

"Yes. And for you. It's going to be the best summer ever."

"Will we see otters?"

"Unlikely, but possible." Mum never answered questions like that with "yes" or "no." She was a scientist, and that meant leaving room for the impossible. "Though I'll be traveling north, out to the Norwegian Sea. There's rumors of a Greenland shark around there."

I hoped for a story, a story about the Greenland shark. She's been telling me about sea creatures since I was little, and I've collected them in this small yellow notebook with a daisy on the front, strung them on a thread like a necklace, each fact shining and precious. But she yawned again, and I could tell from her not using fancy words anymore that she was close to falling asleep.

I rolled over and all I could see were her teeth glinting in the dark. It was like the rest of her face wasn't there and I touched it just to make sure. I can remember her face that night, feel it under my fingers. Words can be time travel, too.

We didn't stay for breakfast at the stuffy B&B, and Dad was very grumpy because Noodle had pooed and it made his pajamas smell. Mum hung them outside the door and closed the window to hold them in place but they escaped on the M5 highway just outside Birmingham and flew under the wheels of a truck. They had a little fight, which took us to the M6 to Manchester, then the M62 past Manchester, then the M6 again.

By this time I was very bored of the M6 and also of the names roads have. Wouldn't it be better if they had names like in books? "Elven-way." "Old North Road," or "Yellow Brick Road"? That would have made the last paragraph a lot more interesting for you and me both.

Two

"Is that it?"

We were sitting in the car on the quay in the village of Gutcher, on the island of Yell, looking at the tiny boat that was going to take us to Unst.

By now we had driven nearly a thousand miles, and had taken one long ferry ride from Aberdeen to Lerwick, a town on Mainland, Shetland. If you still have your map about you, it'll probably be a speck. But it's the biggest speck in Shetland, so that's where the ferries from mainland Scotland arrive.

What I had seen of Shetland so far was very green and very wet, the clouds hanging so low over us I felt sure I could have touched them. Dad unfolded himself from the car as soon as we stopped, and began doing these squat bounces he does every twenty minutes when he's working at the computer. I slid down in my seat, but at least there was no one my age around.

"Sausage roll?" Mum twisted round, holding one out to me. She had a tub of them on her lap, the size of a paint can. She said it's best to buy in bulk if you have to buy plastic. She liked the really cheap, dry sausage rolls where the meat is pink or gray and occasionally you find a little lump that it's best to spit out. Dad says they're made from all the bits they can't sell in a butcher's. He won't eat them.

I took one while Mum stretched in her seat. I heard her neck click. She was used to being outside and moving. She had this really heavy-duty yellow raincoat, the kind oil rig workers wear, and she went out in all weathers. Even when she was on her computer she rested it on the kitchen counter and typed standing up.

"The Greenland shark," I said.

"Mmm?" said Mum, her mouth full of sausage rolls.

"You said about the Greenland shark, at the B&B. Will you find one, do you think?"

Mum chewed thoughtfully, then checked her watch. "Want to stretch your legs?"

"As long as we don't have to stand with Dad."

Now he was swinging his arms from side to side so they hit his bum and legs. I could hear him making little huffing noises even over the wind. Mum snorted with laughter. "Agreed."

We got out and Mum fetched our coats from the trunk. Mine is red, and next to her yellow and Dad's green we look like a set of traffic lights.

The wind nudged us in the direction of a small, drenched bench on the stone quayside. Mum plonked herself down. She doesn't mind being damp: it comes with the territory of being a marine biologist.

"How you holding up, my J?"

"Fine."

"It's been a long journey," she said.

"I know," I said. "I was there."

She looked around and jumped when she saw me, pretending surprise. "So you were!"

I giggled. "The Greenland shark."

"*Somniosus microcephalus.*"

"I've been reading more about it on Dad's phone."

"How did you get signal up here?"

"It says that they live to five hundred and seventeen years old."

Mum shook her head.

"It's not true?"

"It's not proven. It could be true, but they've never found one that old. I think the oldest was about four hundred."

I stared at her. "Four *hundred*?"

"Yep." Mum often did this: dispensed amazing facts like she was reeling off a shopping list. Her knowledge was something she wore as easily as her coat. "There's room for error. Normally with sharks it's easy to age them. Their bones grow rings, like trees. But Greenland sharks, their bones are too soft for that. So they dated the crystals in its eyes."

My brain felt like it was stretching, and I made myself remember these facts to put in my yellow book. "But that's mad!"

Mum flinched. She hated that word. She said mad people were only misunderstood. "It's clever."

"How do they get so old?"

"They're slow," she said. The wind was blowing her hair across her face but she didn't brush it away. I still remember that, how it was loose, though usually she tied it back. That day it half-hid her from sight, so that I thought she looked like a seer from a story, giving prophecy.

"Slow?" I wrinkled my nose. "So?"

"So they move so slowly, they age slowly. They sort of cheat time. They grow one centimeter a year. You know that's this much?" She held up her hand, her fingers nearly touching. "It's not much at all."

"Do you think I'll live a long time, even though I'm growing fast?"

Mum laughed and pulled me to her. She smelled of the rubber of her coat, and of fresh air and sausage rolls. "Of course you will."

"Mu-um." I pretended to try to wriggle free, but really I didn't mind her hugging me. The ferry horn sounded. The boat went very low in the sea once all the cars were onboard, and I tried not to look, taking out my yellow book to distract myself from the idea we might sink. I've been writing in it since I was nine, over a year, and it's full of facts about sea creatures. I turned to a fresh page, titled it *Greenland Sharks*, and added the thing about the crystals, and soft bones.

History isn't my favorite, but I know enough to know that shark was alive before Napoleon was born. Before Mozart, who we learned about in Ms. Braimer's music class. And Napoleon and Mozart were alive a really, really long time ago.

The village of Belmont arrived out of the gray sea and gray clouds, low gray buildings slumped on the shore. I don't mind gray. My favorite animals, other than Noodle, are gray seals. But it did make me feel a bit heavy in my chest, leaving sunny Cornwall and arriving to rainy Unst, even if it was only for the summer.

There was more driving. We were all very quiet, even Noodle, and I wondered if she felt the same as I did. There was one road out of town, and the other cars mainly peeled off until there were two left ahead of us, but they turned right when we forked left at the end of the road, following a print-out of directions Dad had been sent by work. There were no signs, and it got bumpier and bumpier.

The rain tapped on the roof like fingers, like Dad drumming his desk waiting for an email to come. Mum had her window open still and I could smell the rain: mud and grass crushed together.

"Are you sure this is the right way?" said Dad.

"There's no other way to go," said Mum, waving the printout. "It says straight out of Belmont, left at the fork, straight to Uffle-Gent Lighthouse."

Yes, you heard that right. Uffle-Gent. The only other lighthouse in that area was called Muckle Flugga, so it really could have been worse.

The land started rising, and our car huffed its way up, up, up. And when we reached the top, Mum wound her window down lower and stuck her head out and whooped.

"Look, J! Dan!"

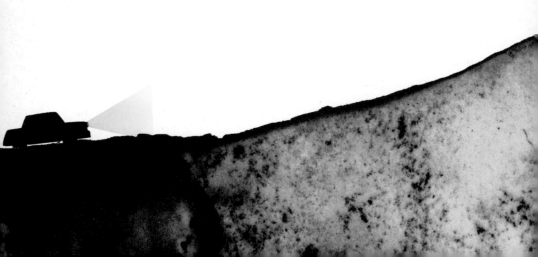

She said it like we might miss it, but it was impossible. At the top of the hill, the road finally flattened out into a scrubby piece of unpaved land, a sort of drive. And arrowing up from the overgrown cliffside, before which was spread a vast and rolling sea, was a round, white-and-black tower.

Uffle-Gent. Our lighthouse.

I could see why so many stories were set in lighthouses. It's a good place for adventures even before you go inside. There was a ladder stretching up the tower, the most direct way to the light. A railing ran along the top, protecting a walkway that wrapped around the light's cage. At the base were tangles of nettles and gorse that Dad had to root through to find the key. He swore a lot and Mum didn't even shout at him, she was so busy looking at the sea. Finally, he found it under an old tin bucket half-full of rainwater. He picked it up gingerly and wiped his fingers on his jeans. He can be a bit of a fusspot, my dad.

Inside was gloomy and cramped, and my heart sort of flip-flopped at the sight of it. You could walk across the whole bottom floor in ten strides, or six of Dad's, and the bathroom was right off the kitchen, the bath and toilet very close together.

The furniture had been left by the last lighthouse keeper, and it did not look happy about it. All the walls were round, and all the furniture was straight-lined so nothing fit, and was placed at right angles like a shipwreck, jutting out and blocking doors. The walls were very thick, but still the damp chased up the sides in dark patches, and the whole place smelled like sea.

The stairway was curled right along the edges of the walls, like an inside helter-skelter. I let Noodle out of her crate and she ran straight up them. We heard her meowing all the way to the top.

"This is going to be an adventure," said Dad.

"A great one," said Mum.

Dad opened his arms and gathered us in so I was squashed between them.

"Let me out!"

They laughed and kissed, so I made a *yuck* sound and followed Noodle up the stairs.

The walls were wet under my fingers and circling around made me dizzy. There were three levels besides the ground floor, all made of wood with big steel struts crisscrossing beneath. There was a double bed in the first one, together with a desk so there was hardly any space to stand.

I continued up. A single bed was on the next level, already made up with musty-looking daisy chain sheets, and a blue lamp on a wooden bedside table. My room. It wasn't anything like at home, with the walls painted like the sea and shells lined up on my shelves. My lip wobbled. It was only a summer, I told myself sternly. That's how long it used to take to sail to Canada from England. A long time, but not a lifetime. And then I'd be home with Shabs, Matty, and Nell again. I went inside and flopped down on the bed. The sheets were damp.

Meowwww.

Noodle was calling me from above. When she gets like that you have to go and see what she wants or she won't shut up. The next level was directly below the light. I could see the cone of glass braced on metal struts hovering overhead, and imagined Dad would set his computer up here, doing embarrassing stretches as he automated the light.

After four days in the car my legs were jelly, and I was breathless by the time I reached the top. Noodle was scratching at a red door with a rusted key in the lock. You couldn't hear the sea or the wind at all behind it. It must be nearly as thick as the wall.

"Mum!" I called down.

Her voice twisted faintly back up to me. "Yes?"

"Can I go outside?"

I already had my hand on the key, but I could hear the hissing sounds of their discussion. Dad was obviously saying no.

"Yes," she shouted after a minute.

"Be careful!" called Dad.

I turned the key, and pushed. The door grated with a sound like nails on a chalkboard, barely moving. I put my shoulder to the metal and leaned my whole weight against it.

It opened, and was caught and swung back suddenly on its hinges by the wind. I slowly forced my way out onto the metal platform, the weather like little slaps on my cheeks,

my
hair turned
to whipping snakes
lashing my face, making my
eyes sting and water.

I wiped them on my sleeve, and the first
thing I saw was not the sea, or the cliff,
or the huge beacon, dim in its metal cage.

The first thing I saw, standing at the
railing, was a boy.

Three

He had obviously been looking out at the sea, and had clearly
not been expecting company. He was a bit shorter than me, and
had thick, black hair like Shabs. It was blowing around his ears,
but I couldn't tell much more about him, because as I opened my
mouth to say *hello*, or *oh*, or *what are you doing here?*, he swung
himself over the railing and disappeared from sight.

I thought he'd jumped, or not been there at all, and my heart
was slippery in my chest, sloshing around in panic. But when
I threw myself at the railing and stared down, there he was,
not splatted in the long grass below, or vanished like a ghost,
but sliding down the rusty ladder on the edges of his sneakers,

his hands safe from the rough surface in gloves. It looked like he was something from a film.

He landed in a superhero crouch, and then pulled a bike out from the overgrown grass and thorns. He leapt on and cycled really, really fast past our car and down the path we'd taken from the ferry. He didn't stop, or look back, and I watched him until his brown coat blurred in the green ground and was gone.

"Julia?"

Mum was standing behind me, her curly hair caught up in one hand to stop it whipping her in the face, her yellow raincoat billowing.

I don't know why I didn't tell her about the boy. Most likely it was because it didn't matter right then, because she reached out her hand to me, and led me back around to the sea-side of the lighthouse.

"That way is Orkney." She pointed. "That way is Greenland." She pointed again. "That way is Norway. And that way is the North Pole."

"Which way's home?"

She grinned down at me, and prodded me in the chest. "Right here. Wherever you are, our Julia."

"Mu-um."

But she was in one of her silly moods and knelt down behind

me, spreading my arms and singing that song that goes all warbly, from that film where the boat sinks and nearly everyone dies. And then Dad was behind her, and they were both singing, and Noodle was in the doorway, looking at us like we were mad. She had a point.

Unpacking didn't take long. Once our old walking boots and brand-new rain boots—green for Dad, blue for Mum, yellow with daisies for me—were unpacked and lined up by the door, the tomato plants ranged on the high, narrow-lipped windowsill in the kitchen extension, it actually already started to feel like home. Mum put some music on her phone, and poured me a big glass of juice.

So long as I didn't think too much about home, I was almost enjoying myself. And there was the mystery of the boy to entertain me. I went outside while Mum and Dad fought over the litter Noodle had been quietly flicking all over the car. They couldn't find a vacuum cleaner in any of the narrow cupboards and Mum started scraping it out with her hands and Dad got funny about germs and *anyway* while they were arguing over microbacterial infection and how cat poo makes you blind, I went to the bottom of the ladder the boy had escaped down, and checked around the grass for clues as Noodle sat on the damp grass, watching me.

The ground was wet and squelchy, and I found a footprint from a sneaker that was slightly smaller than mine. I pushed aside a clump of purply flowers, and underneath was . . .

"Treasure." I held it up for Noodle to look at.

It was a red-and-gold piece of string, the two strands of color wrapped around each other. I could see it had been tied in a knot, and obviously broken off next to it. The ends were frayed and unraveling, and maybe it wouldn't look like treasure to you, but I had a feeling about it, so I pocketed it before going back inside.

That evening it got dark really late because we are so much higher up the world and that means the sun is up for longer. Dad made twirly pasta with gloopy tomato sauce, and lots and lots of grated cheese on top.

We sat around the table, a small scrubbed thing worn smooth from lots of elbows, and I thought about our house in Hayle, which they'd rented out to researchers from Plymouth University for the summer. It felt strange to think of someone else in our house, sitting at our table, using our knives and forks and Mum's shark-print napkins.

Noodle was crouched under the table too, eating her favorite food, albacore tuna in oil, which is a very fancy kind. I don't know what it tastes like because Dad only buys it for Noodle. I don't like tuna much since Mum left out one of her science magazines, and I read an article about how fishing with nets kills loads and loads of other sea animals we don't even eat, like dolphins, and even though it's probably unfair to tuna to not mind as much about them getting caught in nets, I do.

Cats don't care about that sort of thing, though. Noodle would probably eat a dolphin if she could fit her mouth around one.

When we were finished, Mum and I washed up while Dad tried to tune the tiny, box-like telly on the kitchen counter. We didn't have one at home, so even this prehistoric model was a treat. There was no dishwasher here though, and no washing machine either.

"How will we wash our clothes?" I asked.

"There's a laundromat in town," said Mum. "But we can wash Dad's underpants in the sink for now."

"Yuck!"

The sink was tiny and enamel, and we could only do one plate at a time. I dried them up as Mum passed them to me, and put them straight away as there wasn't room for a drying rack.

"They must have been very tidy, the people who lived here before," I said.

"Person," said Mum. "The lighthouse keeper lived here alone."

I thought of the single room with its neat sheets, and wondered if he'd hoped for visitors. "Not even a cat?"

There was a clatter and Dad did a swear, immediately followed by, "Sorry! 50p!" which is meant to mean he puts 50 pence in a swear jar that I get to keep, but my parents stopped actually putting money in the jar when I made £32.50 last summer, and Mum said I was profiteering.

"Is that another 50p I heard, darling?" called Mum.

"No, *darling*," replied Dad. "But it would help if you could look for the remote."

We played the board game Ludo instead.

Four

One evening was all Mum needed to settle in. Perhaps it was because she loved being on the sea, which was always changing anyway and never the same water under you, that she managed to feel at home wherever she was. That is why she was what Dad called confident, and I called nuts. She just didn't care that much what other people thought.

So when she picked her yellow sweater and waterproof yellow trousers, along with her yellow raincoat to take me into town for the first time, she wouldn't have worried that she looked like a banana on the loose. But I was a little less excited about meeting our new neighbors accompanied by a human-sized fruit.

"Where first?" said Mum brightly, grinning over at me. "Shops? Or shops?"

"Shops."

"Good plan, Batman," said Mum, throwing the wheel left as we reached the end of the fork. I gritted my teeth and closed my eyes. She drove very fast.

Within minutes, we reached the town, strung out beside the sea. All the houses were built square and low, like our kitchen, painted white with gray slate roofs, and doors of yellow or red. They reminded me of seagulls, hunkered down along the stone quay.

Mum parked on the road outside a shop called GINLEY'S, which had fruit and vegetables outside, and fishing line and spades in the windows.

"Shall we look for a remote?" said Mum. "And we can buy some apples at the same time!"

"We have apples," I said, remembering the full fruit bowl in the middle of the too-small table.

"But *they* have apples. Let's get a remote and some apples at the same time because we can."

Mum liked to seize the day. I loved that about her.

There weren't many people out, but those that were passing when we got out of the car stopped talking and looked at us. It wasn't unfriendly, more curious, but it still made me go prickly under the collar of my coat. Mum gave them a cheery wave as we walked into Ginley's, and they waved back. I pushed my hands into my pockets and watched my feet.

The shop had a bell that the door knocked when it opened, like Mrs. Gould's Greengrocer in Hayle. It made me feel more at home, though Ginley's was nothing like Mrs. Gould's. That was full of floral aprons and ceramic fish, nothing you could actually need. But Ginley's had superglue and rope, chocolate bars and mealworm bait. Useful things. I liked it.

"Hello," said a cheery voice with a strong Scottish accent. You know how earlier I was saying there's all that room in words? Well, there are whole houses in accents. The man behind the counter had a white beard and very red skin on his nose and cheeks, sort of polished looking like well-loved boots. When he smiled at me, his blue eyes all but disappeared.

"You're new," he said. "The lighthouse?"

"My husband's working on it," said Mum. "But I'm Maura, and I'll be going out with the Norwegian ship."

"*The Floe*?" He rubbed his thumb across his red forehead. "Nice boat. After whales?"

"And other things," she said, patting me on the shoulders. "And this is Julia."

"Nice to make your acquaintance, Julia. I'm Gin."

He said it like the *g* in *penguin*, rather than Mum's favorite drink.

"I have a grandson about your age. Adrian. He's in bed but come back later and I'll introduce you. What can I help you with?"

Mum explained about the remote while I walked the line of sweets in jars. They had those jelly foods in miniature: hot dogs and burgers, even a whole breakfast with bacon and eggs and fried toast, but I knew better than to ask Mum to buy me one. She didn't like individually wrapped sweets, which meant we always bought the huge jars of them. It worked out better all around.

"Remote and apples obtained!" Mum stood behind me, grinning broadly as she balanced her purchases in her arms. "Gin's told me where we can find the library, too."

"See you soon, Maura, Julia," said Gin, nodding his goodbye to us as Mum attempted to open the door with her elbow, dropping apples all over the floor.

"Don't tell Dad," she said, scooping them into the tote I fetched her. "He'll get up in arms about microbial bacteria."

She blew on an apple and took a large bite, chewing and offering it to me. I shook my head. I'm somewhere in between Mum and Dad on things like germs. I wouldn't eat it off the floor like that, not without washing it. But Mum always seemed a bit invincible. Or at least, that she had better things to do than worry. She dumped the apples and remote into the car trunk, and picked up another tote bag.

"Shall we head to the library? We should have brought your dad's underpants."

I snorted. "What?"

She took another bite of the apple and spoke with her mouth full. "The laundromat is the library, too. Come on."

We crossed the road and carried on towards the sea. We passed a fish and chip shop, and a newsagent's, before we arrived at the laundromat/library that meant we didn't have to wash Dad's underpants in the sink.

I looked through the big glass window at the front. All the machines were churning round and round, and I couldn't see any books, or anyone inside except a bored-looking girl behind the counter.

She was older than me, maybe fifteen, and pretty. She had a very long, thick black braid over one shoulder, and a gold nose ring that glinted against her brown skin. She glanced up. I did my most grown-up nod at her and she raised a perfect eyebrow and nodded back. I felt, briefly, very cool.

"Here we are!" Mum pulled me inside. My feeling of cool evaporated as I tripped a little on my shoelaces. The air was humid, like a greenhouse, and I instantly began to sweat.

Mum bounded up to the girl. "Hello! I'm Maura, and this is Julia, and we would like to avail ourselves of your library services."

The girl's eyebrow arched again, but she smiled and jerked her head to the small room behind her. "In there."

"Ta . . ."

"Neeta," said the girl.

"Ta, Neeta!"

I tried not to trip on my laces again as we slid past the girl, and into a tiny room lined floor to ceiling with books. On the floor a green rug in the shape of a caterpillar was spread out like a lawn, and double doors at the back led to a small courtyard, where a woman with Neeta's perfect eyebrows was sitting in a faded Winnie-the-Pooh T-shirt. She was reading a book that had a big man holding a small woman, who was fainting and pouting at the same time. She didn't notice us, so it must have been good.

The kids' section was the biggest, with the lower four shelves on the right side packed end to end. There were all the usual series: *Murder Most Unladylike* and *How to Train Your Dragon*, *Horrid Henry* and *Sophie's Tom*. There were also loads of newer-looking books, their spines barely cracked. I slid one off the shelf.

"That's a good one."

I jumped and turned.

"Here," said the voice, and this time I noticed a gap in the far corner where the bookshelves didn't quite meet. There was a little rectangular space left between them and, peering around the corner of one of the bookshelves, was a brown eye with very long lashes.

"It's you," I said, certain, though I could only see a little of his face. "From the lighthouse!"

"Shhh!" The boy jerked his head at me to come closer. I shimmied along on my knees. "That's my mum." He indicated the woman reading the book with the swooning lady. "She doesn't know I go to the lighthouse. She says it's too dangerous."

"It is if you jump off it like you did," I said.

"Shhh!" he said again, looking nervously at his mum. She didn't look scary, with her large brown eyes and Winnie-the-Pooh T-shirt.

"You left this." I pulled the gold-and-red thread out from my pocket.

"My rakhi!"

"What?"

"Rakhi. It's a bracelet my sister gave me." He mumbled this, like he was embarrassed.

"That's nice of her. Was it your birthday?"

"No, just this thing we do. Sisters give their brothers a piece of string, brothers buy their sisters a present. It's not very fair, really."

"It's a nice piece of string," I said.

"Yeah, well, this one's broken now, so I have to put it in the sea. Took long enough. It was so annoying wearing it to school."

"Why?"

"Some of the boys—" he shrugged—"they don't think boys should wear bracelets. But it's a rakhi, so . . ."

He tailed off, like he was caught between embarrassment and pride. Looking at my walking banana of a mother, I felt like I understood.

"Can I come?"

He wriggled sideways out of the gap. He was shorter than me, as I'd remembered from the lighthouse, and thin, with very long fingers. His hair was curly and stuck out around his ears. "Sure."

"I'm Julia."

"Kin." He stuck his hands in his pockets. "Ma?"

The woman in the courtyard *hmmm?*'d without looking up from her book.

"My rakhi broke. Can I go put it in the sea?"

She glanced up, her eyes flicking from him to the broken string to me. "Straight there and back, *beta*."

"Mum, don't call me that," said the boy, shifting from foot to foot.

"Don't call me Mum," said his mum, unconcernedly, turning a page.

"Yes, Ma." He rolled his eyes, more to himself than me. "You going to get that?"

I looked down at the book in my hand. I'd almost forgotten I was holding it. I opened it to the first page. I like books, obviously, because I like words, but only when things happen right from the first page. This one began with a plane taking off over a massive jungle, so I tucked it under my arm.

"Mum, I'm just going with Kin to the quay."

"All right," said Mum, scanning the shelves. "Be careful."

We emerged into the laundromat, and Neeta pulled a big ledger out from under the counter. "You find something you like?"

I held out the book to her.

"We're just going to put this in the sea," said Kin, holding up the rakhi.

"You still owe me a present," said Neeta, taking the book. "I'll write this up."

We crossed the road to the stone quayside. The sea was choppy and blue, buoys bobbing gently up and down like birds. We leaned against the metal railings, and Kin threw the string in the water.

"Is that it?"

"I made a wish," said Kin defensively. He sat on the railing, his legs swinging over the sea.

"Careful, *beta*!" His mum's voice echoed across the road, and he stood up as though electrocuted, glaring over his shoulder. She and Mum were standing outside the laundromat. Neither was looking at us, but mums always have eyes in the back of their heads.

"I told her not to call me that."

"Why does she?"

"It means 'son.'"

I frowned. "You are her son, though?"

"Yes, but it's . . ." He chewed his lip. "Never mind. It's not my name."

"Kin is nice," I offered, because he seemed upset.

"You think?" He didn't quite meet my eye. "It's better than my real name."

"You're not Kin?"

"You have to swear not to tell anyone."

"Pinky swear," I said, waggling my finger at him. He tapped his own pinky against it, looking confused, so I clarified, "I promise not to tell."

"It's . . . Kinshuk." He shuddered.

"I like it."

"It means 'flower.'"

"I like flowers. Don't you?"

"I guess," he said slowly. "But the boys at school say—"

"They don't seem very much fun."

"They're OK," shrugged Kin. "They're just a bit . . ."

37

He tailed off and glanced back at the laundromat. Our mums were laughing now. My mum's snorts carried on the wind. "I should get back."

"Do you think your mum will let you come visit the lighthouse now we're living there?"

"I'll ask," said Kin, looking hopeful.

"Come on, Julia," called Mum, and we crossed back to them. "Meet Vedi."

The woman in the Winnie-the-Pooh T-shirt smiled. "Here's your book, Julia. It's a good one, isn't it, *beta*?"

Kin nodded.

"Come back as much as you can," Vedi continued. "The council says we have to use it or lose it."

"Of course," said Mum. "I'll be in with my husband's underpants soon!"

I waved at Kin, and he waved back. Inside my chest a little bloom opened. Maybe we could make friends, if only for the summer.

Mum pulled me into her side. "Shall we get chips?"

Five

"How are you liking Unst?" said Mum, her mouth full, legs dangling over the side of the quay.

"It's nice," I said, picking out a particularly crispy chip from the bottom of the paper cone.

"Nice is a nothing word," said Mum. "What do you think of it?"

I thought, chewing and then swallowing deliberately so as to set a good example for my mother. "It's friendly. It's gray. It's quiet."

"The gulls aren't," said Mum, eyeing them suspiciously. But they were small, speckle-backed, not the huge, yellow-beaked ones we get in Cornwall that swoop down and steal ice creams, whole battered fillets of fish, and once, Mrs. Gould's Chihuahua.

"Good words. I would add salty."

"That's because of the chips."

"It's because of the sea."

"But the town isn't salty."

"Go lick that wall," said Mum, gesturing at the house behind us. "Bet you the swear jar it's salty."

I looked out to the sea, blowing on a steaming chip to cool it. "How long will it take? To find the Greenland shark."

"Not long," said Mum confidently. "The sightings are recent, and southerly. I wouldn't be surprised if I find one on my first outing."

"Really?"

"Don't get all Dad about it," said Mum, jabbing me in the ribs, and I rubbed the spot, feeling bad for questioning her. "I only have two months, remember, so it'll have to be quick. And the boat I'm going out with tracked one last year."

"Is this to do with your seaweed stuff again?"

"No," said Mum. "This is about Grandma."

"Grandma Penny?"

"No, my mum. Grandma Julia."

I blinked. "What's she got to do with a shark?"

Mum snorted, wiping salt on her jacket. "Dad would say a

lot. But you know she had dementia? Her brain went wrong, and she started forgetting things."

I nodded, mouth full of hot chips. "Nell's grandma has it, too. She wore slippers to our end-of-year concert."

"Well, Grandma Julia had it young. Early-onset, they call it." Her knuckles were white: she was gripping her yellow jacket very tightly. "She was too young. It shouldn't have happened. If there had been a way to slow it down, we'd have had her longer. It was like a fire, the dementia. It swallowed her up, too fast."

Her voice was tight, and I brushed my knuckles against hers. She cleared her throat, and smiled at me. But I could tell she was trying not to cry. "But Greenland sharks, they're slow. They move like glaciers. That's why they live so long."

I knew Mum was making sense to herself. Her brain did these leaps, connecting dots I never knew were there. She was clever like that.

"So?"

"So . . ." Mum's voice was strengthening now, her eyes clear. "They seem to be moving so slowly they can actually slow time down. And some researchers believe that we can find out what causes this, and use it to slow down time for humans, too."

It sounded like something made-up, like something from a

film. But Mum often told me facts that sounded like fiction, facts I wrote down in my yellow book. Some of my favorite ones are:

1. The longest mountain range on Earth is underwater. It's called the Mid-Ocean Ridge (you'd have thought they'd come up with something more exciting), it's 65,000 kilometers long, and it's less explored than the surface of Mars.

2. The Pacific Ocean is wider than the Moon, and has over 25,000 islands in it.

3. There are more stars in space than grains of sand on every beach in the whole wide world.

4. There are more atoms in a glass of water than there are glasses of water in all the oceans on Earth.

5. Turtles breathe through their bums.

She also told me the first shark existed before the first tree existed, so I already knew sharks belonged on the strange facts list. But centuries-old, time-slowing sharks? That was a whole other kind of weird.

"Maybe," she said, in a small voice. "It'll work. And other families won't have to lose their loved ones so soon."

I snuggled into her side. My friends back home thought it was strange how much I loved my mum, how proud I was of her, but you can see why, can't you?

Mum nuzzled me on the head. "Sorry. I didn't know it would come out like that. Words, eh? I just hope the funding comes through."

"Dad could lend you some," I said, remembering him bragging in the kitchen in Cornwall about how much the lighthouse people were paying him.

"Ha! He doesn't have fifteen million pounds, does he?"

I nearly fell off the quay. "That's *mad*."

"Immoral," corrected Mum. "But that's what research like this costs. Anyway, we're a long way off a lab. Got to find the sharks first, find a way of tracking them. Then we can work on ways to extract the cells we need."

"You're . . . you're not going to kill them, are you?"

Mum looked at me, shocked. "No more than I would kill you, or a hundred-year-old oak tree."

I know that sounds a little strange, that she'd equate me with a tree, but really it's a compliment coming from someone like Mum, who really, really loves trees.

"That's partly why it's complicated," continued Mum. "But

the ideas are sound." She inspected the chip paper, checking to see if it was too greasy to recycle. She nodded approvingly at it and put it in her pocket.

"Can I come?" I asked.

"Where?"

"On the boat? I want to help you find the shark."

"Your dad wouldn't like it."

"So?" Mum never usually cared what Dad thought.

She shrugged. "Maybe. Let me get to know them all a bit. Now come on, my jewel, let's get a sparkle on." Which is her horrifying way of saying "get a wiggle on," which is Dad's horrifying way of saying "let's go." Parents were as embarrassing in Shetland as they were anywhere else.

Scraaape.

I woke up, teeth trilling like I'd chewed on foil. It was a sound like metal too—like a blade scratching a surface. I checked my starfish watch. 2:30 a.m.

Scraaape.

Perhaps I was imagining it.

Scraaape.

"Nope," I said aloud. "Not imagining it."

Noodle emerged from the covers and leapt lightly down onto

the floor, her tail fluffed up like a skunk's. She slunk low, and moved silently out of the door.

I took hold of my flashlight and followed, my thoughts galloping. The bedside light's little glow sprawled onto the opposite wall, sending my shadow monstrous, stairs curving up up and down down into the dark.

Scraaape.

I knew I should fetch Mum. What if it was a thief? My heart thudded fearfully.

Noodle mewled from above, and I jumped, the hair on my arms standing up. I shivered, my bare feet cold on the wooden steps. A smaller scratching sound came, and I knew she was trying to get out of the door. I crept up after her, every muscle taut, ready to run.

Scraaaape.

The noise was louder here. Whatever it was really was on the other side. Noodle wiggled her bum, ready to pounce. Seeing her tiny, tigerish form ready to defend me made me feel braver. I placed my hand on the doorknob, and raised the flashlight high. It was rubber gripped, but heavy. I'd dropped it on my foot once and it'd hurt.

Before I could think better of it, I opened the door and charged, Noodle at my heels like a furred cavalry.

Outside, the night was crisp black, hundreds of stars misting the sky, the moon a half slice of silver-white. And there, silhouetted in my raised flashlight's glow, was—

45

"Kin?"

My momentum carried me forwards, right into him. As we collided my flashlight slipped from my grasp and skittered down over the railings to land with a muffled thump in the grass below.

"Ow." He rubbed his forehead, and I noticed he was holding a rope in his other hand. "Careful!"

"Careful?" I half-laughed, relief battering my ribs. "What are you doing here?"

"What I do every clear night," he said. Noodle was sitting by the open door, eyeing Kin warily, like she did to anyone new. Kin eyed her warily back. "Is that yours?"

"She is. Well, Dad says we're hers more than she's ours, but . . ." Kin was looking at me with the glazed expression of someone who was Not One Of Our Own, which is what Dad calls anyone who isn't absolutely nuts about cats. "But anyway," I continued, switching tack. "What're you doing?"

"Trying not to bash this around too much."

He brought the object the rest of the way up and hoisted it with great care over the railing. I didn't think there was much point after the racket he'd made scraping it along the lighthouse, but I didn't say so, too intrigued by what it was.

"A telescope?"

He nodded proudly.

"Can I?"

I reached out. It was as high as Kin, and heavy too, I could tell just from looking. It had three thin metal legs that formed a tripod, and an eye rest cushioned by buttery red leather. The telescope itself was polished brass like our door handles in Cornwall. He bent over the eyehole, and began adjusting the dials that lined the telescope's length. Noodle retreated back indoors, but I stayed, watching him.

"There," he said, ducking back up with a shy smile.

"Look."

I bent over the scope. Glittering, thrown dust was scattered across the dark sky, which I now saw was not black at all but blue, every shade of blue, from the ocean on warm days to the paint Mum used on the bathroom ceiling, stenciling in gold five-pointed stars, like we got at school for good behavior.

But stars are nothing like that. They are white, and bright as magnesium flares from science. They *are* magnesium flares, and a thousand other kinds of gas and sparks, like the lighthouse beam used to be.

"These stars," said Kin. "They've been there millions of years. Millions. My bapi—" He stopped. "My dad. He says they're older than anything we'll ever know, ever touch. And some of them are dead already. But their light keeps going because they're so far away it takes them forever to reach us."

"Dead?" I squinted at them. I had never seen something that looked more alive. I had the same feeling in my brain, the same stretching one I felt when Mum told me a fact I wanted to write in my yellow book. But that was for sea facts only. I had to keep focused if I was going to be a marine biologist like Mum.

"Mmm. Dad says their light will keep coming until long after we die."

"That's . . . nice?" The truth was it made me feel a little sad.

"Forget it," he mumbled, and made as though to collapse the telescope.

"Wait," I said, holding out my hand. "I do see what you mean."

"You do?" He wasn't looking directly at me, but somewhere off beyond my right ear.

"Yeah."

"I thought you might. With your mum being a scientist and all."

"She studies the sea, not the sky," I said. "But that's just as interesting. More interesting," I added loyally.

Kin wrinkled his nose. "More than that?" He gestured at the enormity of the night around us.

"Yes, but *that*," I shot back, pointing at the sea that was murmuring against the rocks below us. "That's where the real secrets are. We know more about stars than starfish."

I could tell he didn't believe me. But I didn't mind. Mum said the most important part of being a scientist is to listen and to communicate, because you never knew when someone else's ideas could make you change your own.

Six

Kin told me to meet him in the laundromat.

"It's just me and Neeta today."

"Are you working there?"

He shook his head. "There's nowhere else to hang out since the council had to close the library."

I wondered why he didn't want to meet at the beach. There were some sea caves nearby I wanted to explore. But seeing as he'd invited me, I thought it'd be rude not to go, and Mum said it was fine as long as I was back for dinner.

I pocketed a bacon sandwich, collected my bike from the stinking boat shed, and pushed off down the road. The cycle got a lot easier once I was off our potholed stretch, and into the paved street to town. It was no busier than the day before. Kin said a lot of the local kids went to the bigger islands or the mainland for summer. But his family always stayed, because "the laundromat was important to the local infrastructure." He'd looked proud when he said this, the way I must when I talk about Mum.

Gin's shop was open, and he was outside stacking some shelves with bait, a bored-looking boy beside him, holding a crate full of cans. Probably Adrian, his grandson. I waved at Gin's back, and the boy glowered at me. It made me wobble, and I had to put my hand back on the handlebars very fast.

Neeta was behind the counter like yesterday, and Kin was sitting on it, swinging his legs. Dismounting, I locked my bike to a lamppost and waved through the glass. He hopped down and stood in the open doorway.

"You came," he said, sounding a bit surprised. "It's a bit loud."

He wasn't wrong. The machines rumbled and churned like miniature cyclones, nearly all of them going except one with an "out of order" sign stuck to it. Neeta looked up from her phone and did her grown-up nod at me. "Hey."

I nodded back, and squeaked, "Hi." She really was very pretty.

"Can you guys watch it here for a bit?" She stepped out from behind the counter and stretched. "I'm just going to Laura's."

"Sure," said Kin, climbing back onto the counter. Neeta

left, her thick braid swinging, and I watched her go with open awe.

"She's so pretty."

Kin wrinkled his nose. "The boys at school say so. It's gross."

I plonked our laundry bag down on the bench and hopped onto the counter beside him. Kin kicked his heels. "I didn't think you'd come."

"Why?"

He shrugged, but I could tell he did care really because he wasn't looking at me. "I thought you'd think it was weird, hanging out here."

It wasn't the time to mention that I did, a bit.

"Where are your parents?"

"Mainland," he said. "Need new parts for that." He pointed at the broken-down machine.

"And they let you and your sister run the shop?"

"And the library. They used to let me watch it on my own, sometimes," he said proudly. "Then . . ." He sighed.

"What?" I asked. I couldn't imagine Kin trashing the place.

"Just some boys at school. They sometimes come in here."

"To ask Neeta out?"

"Ew, no!" He scrunched his lip up under his nose. "Just, they aren't nice to me."

I nodded, to show I understood. I was bullied for a bit last year by some girls in the year above. They'd poke my belly and call me a whale, and Flubber, even though it's blubber that whales have. But telling them this just made it worse.

"Have you told your mum?" I asked, because that's what I did. She went to school the next day and they didn't bully me for the rest of the year, and then went to Year 7 somewhere else.

"No way," said Kin. "But Neeta noticed. She wouldn't leave me here unless I had someone with me. Not that I mind being alone."

I watched him swinging his legs and I felt—not sad exactly, but I could imagine him here, alone. I didn't have a sister or a brother, unless you counted Noodle, which we do but most people don't, so I was used to being on my own. I didn't mind, and maybe it was like that for Kin, too. But I felt like his words weren't telling the whole story. That he'd been more than alone. That he'd been lonely.

"Are you OK?" He'd looked up suddenly, and seen me watching him.

"Yeah, why?"

"You look like this." He did a funny face, like Noodle when she needs a poo.

"That's just my face."

"Oh, sorry. Want some?" He pulled out a chocolate bar from his pocket. I took some and brought out the bacon sandwich, squashed from my cycle. When I held it out, he shook his head.

"I'm vegetarian."

"My mum is too, mostly."

"Mostly?"

"She does really like bacon. And sausage rolls."

"Right. Pigs then?"

I nodded. "She's sad about it, because pigs are really intelligent."

"So why doesn't she not eat them?"

"I guess she likes the taste too much."

We ate in silence, watching the washers going round and round. "Are you going to come with the telescope tonight?" I asked at last.

He swallowed and shook his head. "Storm coming."

I chewed the inside of my cheek, trying not to think of Mum going out to sea the next day.

"Day after tomorrow, maybe," he continued. "If it clears up. I'm glad you like it."

"The telescope?"

"And the stars stuff. Neeta thinks it's lame."

"That's because she's your sister," I said wisely. But Kin wasn't listening suddenly, looking at the window. It was like watching Noodle when she saw another cat. But instead of puffing himself up like she did, Kin seemed to shrink.

I followed his gaze. The boy I had seen helping Gin was standing outside the laundromat, grinning. But it wasn't a nice grin. When I looked up his smile widened, and he pressed his red face to the window, breathing on the glass. I could feel Kin trembling.

"Is that Gin's grandson?"

But Kin didn't answer. It was like he was under a spell as the boy dragged his finger through the misted-up glass, his floppy blond hair making his face go in shadow. Then he waved, and sauntered out of sight.

Kin wilted next to me, breathing out in a great *whoosh*.

"Was that Adrian?"

"Yeah. The boys at school I told you about. He's their leader, sort of."

I jumped off the counter, and inspected the drawing. It was a four-petaled flower. Kin came to my shoulder. "I have to wash that off."

"Why'd he do that?"

"My name," said Kin miserably. "He thinks it's funny it means flower."

"That's stupid," I said.

Kin grunted, and went behind the counter, coming back with a spray bottle and cloth. "We're lucky Richard wasn't with him. He might have come in."

"He wouldn't have done anything," I said.

"He might have said something," said Kin. "Something horrid."

"Like what?"

But Kin didn't answer. He went outside, checking left and right, and spritzed the marks away. His lip was wobbling when he came back in to sit on the counter again, and I tried to think of something to distract him.

"So what do you do in summer?"

"What do you mean?"

"For fun," I said.

Kin shrugged, gesturing around. "I usually read or something."

"Do you go swimming, or—"

Kin shook his head. "I can't swim."

I sat up straight. "You live on an island."

"So?" Kin was sitting rigidly again, not looking at me. "You sound like the boys at school. They tried to throw me in, once."

"That's not nice," I said firmly. "But swimming is."

"Vikings couldn't swim," said Kin, jutting out his chin. "They thought it was bad luck to learn, because it meant preparing to sink."

I shifted on the counter. It was cutting into the backs of my legs. I didn't like that. Mum swam brilliantly, like a seal or an otter. But that didn't mean she was going to sink. I laughed away my worry.

"You're not a Viking."

"I could be," said Kin, his voice a little too loud even with the machines going. He looked suddenly upset again. "Why is that so strange?"

"I didn't mean—"

"Everything all right?" Neeta was in the doorway.

"Yeah," said Kin, moving away from me. "Julia was just going."

Hurt jabbed at my chest. I didn't understand. "Kin—"

But he was already pushing open the door to the library. "Bye."

It slammed shut behind him, and I looked at Neeta, who shrugged. Face flushing, I slipped past her and back to my bike. As I clipped on my helmet and started to cycle away, I heard a hoot. Looking over my shoulder, I saw Adrian standing with a group of boys. Their laughter chased me away down the street.

Seven

"What's up with you?" Mum was eyeing me suspiciously.

"Nothing."

"No, something." She always did that. Seemed to see right through me. "Did you and Kin have a fight?"

"Leave her alone, Maura," said Dad. He had a jumble of wires in front of him that the postman had delivered. He was starting work tomorrow, and had already developed a worry line between his eyebrows. Mum had her first day on the boat too, but where Dad seemed tense and quiet, Mum was like a coiled spring, ready to go. "Are you taking Noodle tomorrow?"

I knew he'd asked to distract her, but still I had to bite down hard on the inside of my cheek to ask why I wasn't allowed to go.

I filled a glass of water from the tap. The water here was cloudy but it tasted all right.

"Of course." She reached down and scratched Noodle under the chin. "My little mascot. And tonight you'll be meeting Captain Bjorn Johansson." She said the name in a low, gruff voice. "He's coming for dinner."

Dad stopped rooting through the wires. "What?"

"I thought it was only polite," said Mum, returning to her sea maps. "You don't want your wife off with Bjorn Johansson—" the booming voice again, "—without meeting him surely?"

Dad sighed. He didn't like it when Mum was impulsive, and didn't tell him the plan. "I think Bjorn Johansson is the one who should be worried."

"Cupboard risotto tonight please, chef."

Dad's cupboard risotto is whatever rice we have, cooked in a stock cube and any leftover wine in the house, with tinned peas and anything else from the cupboards. It takes a while for it to come close to tasting good, so I helped Dad clear away his wires so he could start cooking.

He led me up to his office beneath the light. I stared up at it, imagined it lit up yellow and hot.

"Just there, J." I put down my armful where he had indicated. "Cool, isn't it?"

He was pointing at the light. Dad is with electricity like Mum is with the sea.

I smiled, hesitating before speaking. "Dad."

He was rummaging in his desk drawer. "Julia."

"Did you tell Mum I couldn't go with her?"

"What?"

"On the boat. Because if she wants me to, I want to go."

"She didn't say anything to me, J."

I chewed my already sore cheek. "Oh."

Dad was leaning on his desk, looking at me carefully. "Are you all right, J? You do seem a bit upset."

I wanted to tell him about Adrian, and what Kin had said about Vikings not swimming, and how I felt like I'd done something wrong, and I didn't know how to put it right. But then we'd have to have A Conversation, and I didn't really want to.

"Noodle goes on the boat."

"Noodle's Noodle," shrugged Dad, like he was making a valid point. "But we'll have fun, won't we? You can help me with the light." I looked at the wires. Fun was not the word I was thinking of. "And you have your friend. Kevin, is it?"

"Kin." His name stuck in my throat.

"Well, he can come for lunch one day."

I knew Dad wanted to suss him out before letting me hang

around with him, but there was no need. Kin didn't seem to want to be friends anymore. "Maybe."

Mum's voice came from the spiral staircase. "Shall I start chopping?"

"Quick," grimaced Dad, pushing himself off his desk. "Before she butchers herself."

The small kitchen quickly filled with the smell of garlic and wine. Noodle slunk upstairs when Mum added too much chili powder, and by the time there was a knock at the open door we were all red-faced and spluttering.

Mum threw open her arms like she was greeting an old friend. "Captain Bjorn! Welcome! Don't come in, you'll suffocate."

The man outside was tall and thin. His eyes were pale blue and crinkly, his skin very reddish-brown with sunburn at the wrists when he held out his hand to shake Mum's. She hugged him instead, and pushed me forward.

"This is Julia, and that, coughing into the risotto, is Dan."

Dad waved in welcome, eyes watering.

"Very nice to meet you, Julia." His accent was thick and made his words clipped, with odd pauses. It was a nice voice.

"Will you help us carry the table out?" said Mum. "It's not currently habitable in there."

"Might as well make the most of the nice day," said Captain Bjorn. "The weather will turn tonight."

Maneuvering the table through the narrow door gave me a new appreciation for whoever had put it in there. It was only when Captain Bjorn screwed off one of the legs that we managed it, and found a patch of even ground, which happened to be directly below the ladder. I scooped up my flashlight before anyone noticed it, but Mum frowned at the trodden-down scrub, which suddenly looked very obviously like a path.

"Looks like we have visitors sometimes."

"Possibly otters," said Captain Bjorn. "They are busy here."

Dad plonked the cupboard risotto down at the center of the table, and we settled to eat.

Mum, as usual, started the conversation. "What time do we start?"

"Early," said Captain Bjorn. "As long on the sea as possible. There'll be another storm coming westerly midafternoon."

"And we'll lay our markers?"

"Yes."

"And then," said Mum, her mouth full. "Maybe sightings?"

Captain Bjorn shrugged, but it wasn't dismissive. "Maybe next week, maybe next month. Maybe never. They favor the depths."

"That's why you have sonar."

"Of course. I've never seen one though."

"Your crew has?"

"But not me."

"But I will." She grinned at me, saying it definitely, and I believed her. When Mum was certain about something, she was right.

"Maybe," said Captain Bjorn, and I saw Dad look from the captain's face to Mum's, with something like worry in his eyes. "This research, which university is funding it?"

"None at the moment," said Mum cheerily, heaping seconds into his bowl. "Seed money only. But I've got the wheels moving."

Captain Bjorn chewed for a lot longer than the cupboard risotto needed chewing. "Is this why you've only chartered us for two weeks?"

"Two weeks?" I asked. "Two months, I thought."

"Yes." Mum wafted her hand, like it wasn't an important detail. "I'm paying as we go. It'll work out. The money will come. The science is sound." She said these sentences like a mantra, a prayer.

"And what's the science?" he asked. "If you don't mind me asking."

Mum had her mouth full again, so I answered for her.

"The shark can slow time. Mum's going to use it to slow down time for people, too."

"Something like that," said Mum.

Captain Bjorn raised a pale eyebrow. "These sharks, they are not easy to find. It may not be possible."

65

I glared into my cupboard risotto. Who was he, to tell Mum what was possible or not?

"I'm not easy to hide from," said Mum, and there was something in the air there. Something taut, like they both had hold of an invisible rope and were pulling it between them.

"They swim many meters down."

"Over two thousand," shrugged Mum. "But they come to the surface."

"Sometimes."

"Exactly."

Captain Bjorn toppled first, shrugging. "All right."

"It will be," said Mum, unable to resist having the last word.

I felt my own hand clench as hers flexed on the table, and Dad laid his own over it. I shifted in my chair, searching for something to say to puncture the swelling tension.

"Captain Bjorn, can you swim?"

"Of course."

That was something, at least.

After dinner, Mum and Dad had a little fight. I didn't stick around to listen, but I think it was about money. It usually was. I knew they'd borrowed a lot for our house in Cornwall so the bank owned it twice, or something. I forced myself to stay awake, using my facts book to work out that two thousand meters is the height of twenty Big Bens stacked on top of each other.

That's how deep the sharks like to swim. Twenty Big Bens. On top of each other. Under the sea. I felt another needling prickle of worry in my chest that Captain Bjorn might be right, but I forced the thought away. Mum believed, and that's all I needed to know.

Finally, I heard them go to bed, and Mum started snoring. She took pills to help her sleep, but still I crept very quietly upstairs, lifting my slippered feet carefully.

I was already learning the lighthouse, where to step so the stair didn't creak, the slick patches where my slippers had no grip, and it was already becoming less extraordinary to me.

It was the way of things to become ordinary after a while, and that was why I liked what Mum did so much. Instead of things becoming more ordinary the more she looked at them, they became more interesting. Sharks, whales, even algae.

I knew Kin wasn't going to be there. Even if we hadn't fallen out, the clouds he'd mentioned from the storm Captain Bjorn promised were arriving, misting the stars in gray froth. The sea was quiet, and so dark I couldn't see it. It was like there was a pit below me, reaching all the way to the center of the earth, further even than my imagination could reach.

Eight

Mum came back from sea fizzing. Noodle seemed proud of herself too, curled up on Dad's lap so he could brush out the knots in her fur where wind and salt had matted it.

"It's *wild*," said Mum, looking wild herself. She grabbed my hands and spun me around. "The waves were high as this, more than that, and the color!"

She let go and my hip bumped the table sharply. I plonked myself down, wanting, suddenly and stupidly, to cry. Mum didn't notice, chattering on. "So different from Cornwall, a sort of crispness to it. And we saw *Phocoena phocoena*, dozens of *Phocidae*—" she broke off, looking at me expectantly.

"Harbor porpoises, seals," I recited dully.

"Hey, what's up with you?"

I shrugged, one of those shrugs that really means, *Oh, I don't know, Mum, maybe it's that you've dragged me up here away from my friends to the middle of nowhere and you won't even let me go on the boat with you.* Adding to my mood was the fact I'd had a very boring day helping Dad untangle the wires and lay them into rainbow stripes on the floor. All I could think about as I sorted them was how much more fun I could be having with Mum at sea, or even with Kin in the laundromat. But neither Mum nor Kin wanted me.

"What's up with her?"

Dad shrugged too, and I wondered if his meant something more as well.

"You're about as communicative as Bjorn." Mum sighed. "I'll need another layer tomorrow. The storm brought a cold front, but at least it'll be clear."

"Did you see any Greenland sharks?" I asked, and Mum's energy seemed to wilt a little.

"No, but that's to be expected. They're tricky to spot at the best of times." I didn't remind her that's not what she said yesterday. "We weren't far enough north. We're mapping at the moment, to track their movements. We'll find one, I'm sure. It's only the first day." She seemed to be talking to herself more than us. "And this means I can write to the university again, and tell them we've started. They'll have to give us the funding now we're actually out there. I'll need a new camera at least, to document everything."

Dad's forehead creased. "I thought you'd basically secured the money already."

Mum waved her hands, wafting his comment away. "This sort of research, it's not been done before. There's no precedent. We'll need to train people."

Dad nodded slowly. "How long is this going to take?"

"As long as it takes."

"Julia has school, and I'll be done in two months—"

"And I might be done then, too. Or in three. This is a once-in-a-lifetime opportunity, Dan, and—"

"Maura." Dad flicked his eyes to me, like I was still little and wouldn't notice they were already fighting.

"I might go read," I said, and before they could stop me I picked up my library book and climbed the snail shell staircase, Noodle running ahead of me. I threw myself onto the bed, trying not to listen to Mum and Dad hissing at each other below me, and reached under my pillow, pulling out my yellow notebook.

Noodle curled onto my lower back as I turned over a new page and split it into three columns. I wrote the date and the number of hours Mum had been at sea in the first two, and then harbor porpoises and seals in the third. Chewing my pencil, I considered the page and then, feeling a little traitorous, drew a fourth, very skinny column and put an X in it. Tomorrow it would be a check. I had to believe it as hard as Mum, or else I'd be letting her down as badly as Dad.

I turned a new page. I wanted to write down what Kin had told me about the stars, and about Vikings. But we weren't friends anymore, and they weren't strictly sea creature facts, which is what my yellow book is for. I sighed and put it away. You have to have some rules, like gravity. Otherwise you could float right off the edge of the world.

When Mum and Dad finally went to bed, I picked up my rescued flashlight and pulled on a sweater. Noodle followed until she realized I was going up, not down to feed her. She mewed pitifully, but I ignored her. Nerves fluttered in my belly, though there was no reason for it. It was my lighthouse. I lived here, even if it was only for a summer. I could go outside if I wanted.

But Kin wasn't there. The narrow passage around the blank beam was empty. I walked around it once to make sure, then slumped down beside the door, telling myself I didn't care. In two months I'd be home in Hayle, and I wouldn't even remember Kin, or the lighthouse. But—and this felt like a bad thought, a thought that made me feel a bit sad—my friends from home didn't care about the things I cared about.

Remember the whale, who went around the world on the wrong frequency? Sometimes, when they were talking about YouTubers or making up dance routines, I felt like that whale. Like they could see me, but not hear me. And Kin—I think he was the same, from what he'd said about the boys at school. It sounds stupid, I know, but I thought I'd found someone on my frequency. And then I ruined it, and I didn't even understand how.

The next morning a parcel arrived for Mum while we were having breakfast. When the knock came it wasn't the usual postman, but a man in a smart red and yellow uniform.

"Brilliant," beamed Mum, as she signed for the package, her mouth still full of scrambled eggs. "Worth every penny!"

"What is?" asked Dad, his worry line back between his eyes.

"The guaranteed delivery," said Mum, cheerily waving the deliveryman off and brandishing the package at us before pushing aside Dad's cereal bowl and sending soggy cornflakes sloshing. "I needed this to arrive before I left."

She attempted to get through the packaging, hacking unsuccessfully with a butter knife until Dad handed her the kitchen scissors. His worry line was deep as the Mariana Trench (the deepest place in the world, so not literally, obviously) as she lifted a neat white box with a photo of a black camera on it.

"Ta-da!" She held it out to me. "Look, Julia! All the best wildlife photographers use these."

"But you're not a wildlife photographer," said Dad.

"No, but I do need to photograph wildlife," said Mum breezily, as I opened the box and pulled the camera from its casing. It had three lenses and was black and very shiny.

"Did you get your grant then?" I said excitedly, remembering how she'd said a camera would be first on her list when she did.

"Honestly, Julia," said Mum, snatching the camera from me a little too roughly. "You sound like your dad. This is an investment, see? I have to go charge it before I leave. Excuse me."

She dashed out of the kitchen, and I blinked very fast to hide that I was about to cry. I hadn't meant to burst her excitement bubble.

"It's OK, Julia," said Dad, but the way he said it sounded like the opposite.

After she'd charged her new camera, Mum left for an overnight voyage, which meant I wouldn't be able to focus on anything all day, and meant Dad cradling the radio they used to communicate like a baby to his chest. That night I waited until I heard his door close, and snuck back up to the platform.

The hope was smaller this time, but still it stung a little when Kin wasn't there. In Dad's sternest voice, I told myself I didn't need him. I had Noodle, and Dad, and a mum who was doing important, lifesaving research. I could cope for two months in a strange place with no friends.

It was very cold on the platform, the sky even brighter than the first night. Kin would love it. I shook my head to loosen the thoughts of him. Really, it was good he wasn't here. I could get a decent night's sleep, and maybe Mum would let me go on the boat next time—

"Hi."

Kin's head was hovering on the other side of the railing.

"Hi," I said back casually.

"I'm coming up," he said. "Catch."

He threw a rope to me, impressively accurately. It was rough and strong in my hands. The telescope rope.

I watched him wordlessly as he leaned over the railing and started drawing it up, heaving it over the metal and adjusting the tripod.

He looked through the lens, moving the telescope slightly until he found what he wanted, tightening the screw to hold the telescope in place. My heart was drumming hard, and just as I was about to give in and say *sorry* or *I'm glad to see you* or *did you know Greenland sharks smell of pee*, he turned.

"Come on then."

Careful not to grin, I stood, and went to look through the lens. The buttery leather was soft against my cheek, and the slice of sky I could see was so beautiful I sighed before I could stop myself. He had focused it on the North Star.

"See it?" asked Kin. "Dhruva Tara?"

"Bless you."

He narrowed his eyes. Again I had the feeling of saying something wrong, and zipped my lips up tight. "It's the Dhruva Tara. That's what my dad calls it."

He was looking at me very intently, his face illuminated in the starlight. It seemed like this was a test, a test I was desperate to pass.

"I like it. What's it mean?"

"Dhruva was a king. Tara means star."

Carefully, I nodded. "My mum calls it the North Star."

Something shifted in his face, like clouds parting. He grinned. "Yes. They're both names for it. The Vikings called it the lodestar. Other people call it Polaris."

"What do you call it?"

"Depends if I'm feeling more like my dad or a Viking."

I nodded, understanding. "Tonight?"

"Both." He scuffed his foot on the metal platform. "Julia—"

I knew he was about to say sorry, but I didn't need to hear it. "Me too," I said.

Still addressing his feet, he said, "Adrian and the others, they said this island was for Vikings, and that I couldn't be one, because my parents are from India, and I have different names for things. But things have lots of names. Even me."

"Like stars," I said. "I wasn't saying you couldn't be a Viking."

"I know," he mumbled. "I just got . . ."

He tailed off, but I already knew what he was talking about, the way feelings get bunched up under your rib cage and tear out all spiky.

"That's why I was here, the day you arrived," he went on. "I used to go to the beach, but they hang out there. They tease me about the swimming."

"Have they been to the laundromat again?"

He nodded miserably. "And when I went cycling the other day, Adrian came right at me. I fell off trying to avoid him."

He held up his hand, a scrape mark clearly visible on his palm. Anger spilled hot as tea inside me. "Didn't you tell your mum?"

"No way! And you can't either. Promise?"

I promised, but his face was crumpled like a piece of old tissue. He looked up at the stars. "I wish I could see these all the time. I wish it was always dark, and clear."

I looked back through the telescope. A thought arrived bright as Polaris.

"Kin," I said, straightening. "My mum has a spare camera. A really good one that she doesn't take out with her on the boat because it's not waterproof. We could take some photos of the stars."

He was already nodding. "Now? We won't have a night this clear again for ages."

I crept back inside, keeping to the edges until I reached Mum's desk. I found the old camera in the top left drawer, and brought it back up to Kin. "Here."

I turned it on. The memory card was full so I deleted some photos of a field with some sort of swarm over it, and aligned the lens to the telescope. Keeping very still, I pressed the shutter. The first photos were blurry and I had to keep deleting and retaking them.

"Let me try," said Kin. His came out better, and we flicked through, him telling me the different names for each bright speck.

My teeth started to chatter. The clear night meant it was so cold I could see my breath, misting the air like the stardust. Kin was shivering, too.

"You should go," I said. "We'll dress warmer next time."

"Next time?" He smiled. "You sure?"

"Of course," I said. "And if you don't want to go to the beach or hang around the laundromat, you can come here. My mum's out on the boat all the time and my dad is just sorting out wires."

He looked up at me, uncertain. "You really don't mind?"

I nudged him with my elbow. "I want you to."

He smiled then, a proper smile that stretched his cheeks wide. "All right."

I watched him climb down, and lowered the telescope after him. Before I went back inside, I flicked through the photos again, whispering the names of the constellations he'd taught me. *Cassiopeia. Jasi. Sarpa, Ursa Major.* Just because they couldn't go in my yellow notebook didn't mean I wanted to forget them.

I was just about to turn the handle when the door was flung open with a grinding sound. Dad stood in the doorway, hands on his hips, the radio blinking at his hip.

"Julia Ada Farrier. Just what do you think you are doing?"

Nine

Dad bundled me straight into a hot bath, muttering about pneumonia and how I was just like my mother.

"Anything on the radio?" I asked, my teeth chattering.

"Nothing," said Dad, a little too brightly. "But she said that would be the case. They're further north than yesterday. So don't you worry." He rattled on before I could tell him I wasn't worried. "So are you and Kin friends again?"

"How did you know we weren't?"

"I might be your dad, but I still notice things." He smiled. "Next time you go adventuring, wear a sweater."

"We weren't adventuring. We were stargazing."

"Wear. A. Sweater." He picked up the camera from where I

had laid it on the sink. "And be careful with this, J. You can use my camera if you like."

"I *was* careful."

"I know," he said soothingly.

"She has that new one now anyway."

"Yes," said Dad. "Though I'm going to talk to her about sending it back. I looked up the model and . . ." He sighed. "Anyway. It's extravagant. But this one," he brandished the camera, "is special. So we're going to leave it to Mum, OK?"

"OK."

He left me to wash, both the radio and the camera now cradled to his chest. Noodle came to sit on the edge of the bath, straight-backed like it was the prow of a boat.

"Are you sad Mum left you behind too?" I asked her, and she blinked mournfully at me. The water further north was too rough to take her, which meant really Mum shouldn't be going either. But I comforted myself with the fact Captain Bjorn seemed sensible.

I thought about what he'd said, about never seeing a Greenland shark himself. How Mum might not find one at all. The shadow that had moved under Mum's face when he said it, like a fin cutting just under the surface of water. It had been exactly like Kin's expression when he'd seen Adrian at the laundromat window.

I shuddered, the water suddenly feeling as cold as outside.

Noodle batted at the bubbles, but I couldn't relax, and I got out. I changed into clean pajamas, and Dad came down from his office to tuck me in, layering an extra blanket on top of my duvet.

"How's the light thing going?" I yawned.

He chuckled. "You really are like your mum. You know the Latin names for sea creatures and yet you still call my work 'the light thing.'" I smiled proudly as he rubbed his eyes with the heels of his hands. "Not easy, not like I hoped. But I'll make it work." He stroked back my hair. "Go to sleep, J."

It was easier said than done. The wind picked up, and soon it was howling, making the lighthouse creak and pop, like trodden-on floorboards, whipping the smell of grass and salt through the gaps of my door. The sea was the worst, though, so loud, roaring like a monster. I half-expected it to seep through the walls. I took hold of my yellow notebook for comfort. The rough seas had reached us,

and I hoped Mum

was

holding

on

tight.

The bed was a boat, and the sheets
turned to foam under my fingers.
The whole room was rocking, and
above me the roof was gone, replaced
with lightning lashing the low, thick
clouds, long tongues of fire furling and
unfurling, tracing veins of burning silver—
but silent. It raged and raged, without
a sound.

And there was something in the water.

It was deep,

moving slowly

through the black sea.

The water rose above the rolling shape,

huge and swallowing as the sky.

I couldn't move,

couldn't see it.

It was quiet, all so quiet

I felt caught behind glass.

I couldn't turn my head,

but I knew it was rising,

knew it was opening

a mouth

wide as

the world—

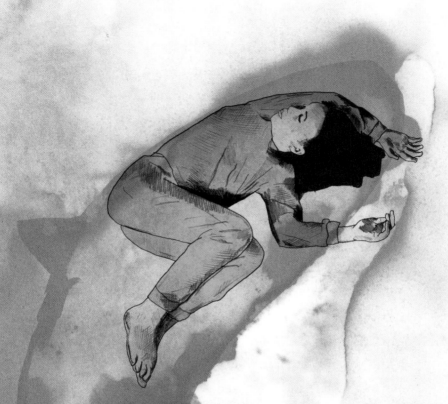

Wailing woke me. I lay still, heart beating too fast from my nightmare, until I recognized it as the screeching of the kettle, boiling on the stove. I squinted at my watch. 3:23 a.m. I sighed, and rolled over. Dad had clearly not been able to sleep after all.

Then I realized he was talking, a low rumble. But it was not Noodle's answering squeak that came next, but Mum's voice, quiet and fast. Relief spread warm through my body, and I swung my legs out of bed. She would come in to kiss me like she always did, but I wanted to hear how it had gone.

I started down the stairs when there was a thump, a bang as though something had been slammed on the table. I stopped short and sat down on the stairs, breathing quietly.

"Complete waste of time," came Mum's voice, floating in and out of listening level. I crept down another step. "I said he was being too careful—"

"No such thing as too careful," said Dad soothingly. "He knows what he's doing."

"Or he's taking advantage," said Mum. "He knows we don't have the budget at the moment, and the grant application won't be processed for days."

"He has to make a living—"

"Whose side are you on?"

"You're not being fair, Maura—"

A bang again, and I realized Mum was hitting her hand on the table. Noodle shot up the stairs, coming to a halt next to me, rubbing against my knee.

"No, *you're* not being fair," Mum sounded even angrier. "You know what this means to me. If I could just get someone to believe in me—"

"I believe in you. Julia does. Your mum did."

There was a gasp, and soft sobs that scared me almost as much as the ferocity had. Mum was crying. The noise made a lump swell in my throat. I felt like I'd heard her cry like that before, but I couldn't remember when.

"Shhhh," said Dad gently. "It's all right. You mustn't get like this, Maura. You know what happened before."

"I won't. I'm not—I'm sorry. I just want this to work, Dan. I need this to work."

"And I know you'll do everything you can. But your health is more important. Are you taking your pills?"

"I know that." The impatience was back in Mum's voice, and she ignored Dad's question. "I don't want to talk about it anymore if you're going to patronize me."

There was a scrape as Mum pushed her chair back. I scuttled around the curve of the staircase, leaping into bed just as I heard her footsteps on the stair outside.

But though I heard her pause outside my room, she didn't come in.

She pulled the door closed, softly, and I lay in the dark, listening as she went back down, the floorboards of their bedroom creaking as she got into bed. The kettle was still screaming. It leveled off into a low whistle as Dad lifted it off the stove. I pulled out my yellow notebook and put another cross into the fourth column.

Ten

Our new life found its rhythm. Kin came to visit most days, and we'd talk about books and stars and the sea. I'd try to get him to talk about Adrian, but he refused. I understood, sort of. When I was bullied it made me feel sticky and gross, like a slug, and it took me ages to tell anyone.

Dad would clatter about the light, squeezing past us on the balcony with wires, swearing and shouting "Swear jar!" by turns, and Mum was hardly ever home.

She stayed away for nights at a time while her two weeks with Captain Bjorn ticked down. I didn't hear any more arguments, even about the expensive camera, but maybe it was only they had them more quietly.

Kin and the stars were almost enough of a distraction from

Mum's leaving, and I was getting good at remembering the star names. He was teaching me about quadrants, and how the same star sometimes had a hundred different myths. In return, I was telling him about my mum's research, which sounded as far-fetched to him as his stories did to me.

"A shark, older than trees?" He shook his head. "And she's going to stop people dying with it?"

"Not exactly," I said. "She's trying to slow down aging. My grandma was sick, and she died before they could find a cure."

"I'm sorry," said Kin. "It's nice your mum is doing something for her. Have they found one yet?"

I shook my head. It seemed to be going better since the first failed overnight expedition. They were away for days at a time, covering vast distances, stretching all the way into the Arctic Circle and beyond.

"It's so beautiful, J," she'd sigh. "I'll take you someday."

I'd bite my tongue, holding in my question of why she could not take me this moment, now, the very next day. But though Mum came home with photos on her new camera of orcas and humpback whales, seals and porpoises, sea ice and every kind of seabird, there was hardly any mention of the shark.

The truth was that when Mum was at the lighthouse, she wasn't exactly easy to be around. One morning she got back so late it was daytime, and Dad and I went to the big supermarket on Mainland, Shetland, to get a tub of her favorite sausage rolls. We made a bow for it out of old newspaper, setting it on the table so it would be the first thing she saw when she got in. We even set the table with knives and forks, so it was like a proper party.

But when the key turned in the lock, Mum barely seemed to notice us, let alone the sausage rolls. Her eyes had huge dark smudges under them like storm clouds, and there was an unsettling energy around her too, like the approaching crackle of lightning. It reminded me of how Noodle gets sometimes, chasing shadows and things that aren't there, but it's a lot less cute when it's your mum. Her round face was thinner, more straight-lined, like the furniture in the curved rooms of the lighthouse. Like she wasn't fitting her skin.

"Hey little J, missed me?" She hugged me, and she smelled of the sea. I nodded into her coat, the rubber making small squeaking noises, and tried to ignore how I could feel the bones in her back, when usually she was lovely and soft.

I didn't need to ask if she'd found the shark—I could feel from her hug that she wasn't happy. She hugged Dad too, but instead of sitting at the table with us she picked up the giant tub of sausage rolls from the table, seeming not to notice the bow as it peeled off, and went upstairs, muttering about work.

"Never mind, J," said Dad bracingly. "Pasta?" But I suddenly didn't feel hungry.

That evening wasn't much better. She emerged for dinner so late it was almost fully dark outside, talking about sightings on Norwegian fisherman forums, and grant applications, and not at all about me or Dad.

Her brain was obviously still at sea, searching for the shark, and when she did eventually ask me questions, her eyes were sort of glassy and far away. I knew she was brilliant, and that her brain was very clever, but she wasn't good at focusing on more than one thing at once.

We had a few nights like this, and every few days a thin white envelope would arrive with Mum's name on it: Dr. Maura Farrier.

The first time, Mum had ripped it open at the kitchen table.

"It's here, Dan, look!" But she fell silent, and read the brief contents with her lips pressed tight together. She scrunched up the piece of paper, and threw it on the wood burner where it crumpled up to ash.

"No?" said Dad tentatively.

Mum shook her head. "Plenty more fish in the sea."

And even I laughed, because she hadn't made one of her stupid jokes in a long time, and I'd missed them, even though they were terrible. When more envelopes came, though, they were no thicker than the last. After the third one, Mum didn't even open them in front of us.

Two weeks after we arrived in Unst, I was writing in my notebook when Mum came through the door with an armful of flowers, a bottle of wine under the other.

"Where's your dad?" she said, planting a kiss on the top of my head. Without waiting for a response, she leaned up the stairs and shouted. "Dan! Dad! The girls require your presence!"

Noodle came running downstairs at the sound of her voice, and Mum scooped her up and plonked her onto the table.

"What's going on?" I snatched up my notebook as Mum scattered the flowers over it and Noodle. She always refused extra packaging, even when it wasn't practical.

She rattled about in the kitchen drawer, finding a corkscrew. "We are celebrating!"

"Celebrating what?" Dad was standing on the bottom step, eyeing Mum warily. She pulled the cork out with a flourish, even though it was only just after lunchtime.

"Progress!" She slopped three glugs of wine into three glasses.

"The grant?" Dad stepped forward, relief plain on his face, but Mum waved his question away.

"Much better." She put the glasses down in front of us, and Dad surreptitiously poured mine into his glass as Noodle sniffed it and, realizing it wasn't something she wanted to drink, jumped off the table.

"The shark?" I clapped my hands. "You found the shark!"

"Soon," she said, raising her glass in a toast and looking around at us both triumphantly. "I bought a boat!"

She drank a big gulp of wine, her swallowing the only sound in the silence.

"A boat?" I repeated, saying it slowly to give my brain time to catch up.

"Maura," said Dad faintly. "What do you mean?"

"What I said, silly!" Mum poured more wine into her glass, and I saw her hands were shaking. I moved my notebook out of the way to stop it from getting splashed, watching her nervously. "Captain Bjorn said he couldn't wait any longer for the grant to come through, and so I thought, why not get my own boat?"

"Because," said Dad, "we can't afford it."

But Mum ignored this, chattering on with a strange brightness in her too-wide eyes. I clamped my hands under my armpits, hugging myself and breathing slowly, like that might calm her down, too.

"I can sail just as well as him," she said, "and it'll work out cheaper in the long run. Gin had his old fishing boat just rotting away, and I have the transmitters from Falmouth, and the radar, and it won't take a week for me to get everything ready. I'll need your help, of course, and Julia can do some of the mending, if you want to, J? Kin can help, too." She looked at me expectantly.

Dad sat down heavily, and reached for Mum's hand. "I'm not sure—"

She snatched it away. "I'm going to email the uni now, and tell them the new plan." She smiled brightly at us both, and disappeared upstairs. I looked to Dad, expecting a reassuring remark or a rueful grin, two of his usual reactions to Mum's plans, but his face was creased with worry. I squeezed my arms tighter.

"Give us a minute, J," he said, and, without looking at me, he followed Mum up the stairs. I didn't want to listen to another argument. Loosing my hands, I snatched up my yellow notebook and slid it into my pocket.

"I'm going to see Kin," I called, and without waiting for an answer I went to the shed for my bike.

My thoughts cycled hard as my legs. The brightness of Mum's eyes, the worry in Dad's voice, and in my chest the increasing feeling of nervousness whenever we talked about the shark. At the beginning, that hadn't been there at all. In the beginning, I had been as excited as Mum. But her excitement had an edge to it now, like desperation.

It was strange, but somehow familiar, like I'd seen her like this before. The memories were fuzzy like someone had rubbed

Vaseline on my brain. Under all this was the worst thought: the traitorous thought. That maybe Dad was right about the boat being a bad idea. Which meant Mum was wrong.

My legs and lungs were burning by the time I reached town, and from the heat in my face I knew I was red as the tomatoes growing on the windowsill. So when I rounded the bend to town, and saw Adrian and two other boys cycling towards me, I kept my head very low down and wished to be invisible, like I had been to Dad at the table. It didn't work.

"It's Flower's girlfriend!" Adrian swerved in front of my bike, and I had to brake very hard.

"She's twice his size," snorted one of his friends.

"Isn't your mum a whale scientist?" said the other, a tall boy with curly hair. "Is that why she had you?"

I glared at him, pulling my jeans up higher where they had slipped down as I rode. "She's a marine biologist."

Adrian yawned widely, showing gappy teeth. "Don't care."

I put my foot on the pedal, but he didn't move.

"Excuse me," I said in my best Mum voice, the one she uses when someone pushes in front of her in a queue and she wants to sound polite while actually threatening their life. "Let me through."

Adrian got off his bike and wheeled forwards a couple of paces. My heart was beating so hard I was sure he'd hear it. Surely he wouldn't hit me? Not here, on the main street, in the middle of the day? But instead he just walked around me, his wheel almost touching mine.

"Later, whale," he sneered.

I pushed off, being very careful not to look back.

I found Kin in the library room at the laundromat, and his parents let us into their little courtyard at the back and gave us milk and biscuits. I was still shaking from my encounter with Adrian and his cronies.

"We have to do something about them. They can't just go around being like that."

Kin shrugged, his face going closed off like it had when Adrian had come to the laundromat. "You have to just ignore them."

"Bit hard when they're standing in my way. Maybe we should tell Gin—he's his granddad, right?" Kin didn't answer. He obviously wanted me to stop talking about it. I sighed, then snapped my fingers. Mentioning Gin made me realize the reason I'd come to see Kin in the first place.

"Gin's boat?" Kin's eyebrows lifted like two black caterpillars when I relayed Mum's plan. "It's really old."

"She's good at fixing boats," I said. "And she said you can help."

Kin looked unsure. "I'm not sure I'd be any good."

"You've never tried," I said. "It's a useful Viking skill."

His face lit up at that. "Yeah, suppose. What will I have to do?"

They say you can't smell anything in dreams,
but that night the stink of the shark filled my
nostrils. I tried to open my eyes but they were
frosted like glass beneath ice, and every breath
was full of water. The shark was beneath my
bed, growing large as the room, large as the
lighthouse, rising from unfathomable depths
until it ripped the whole island from its roots.

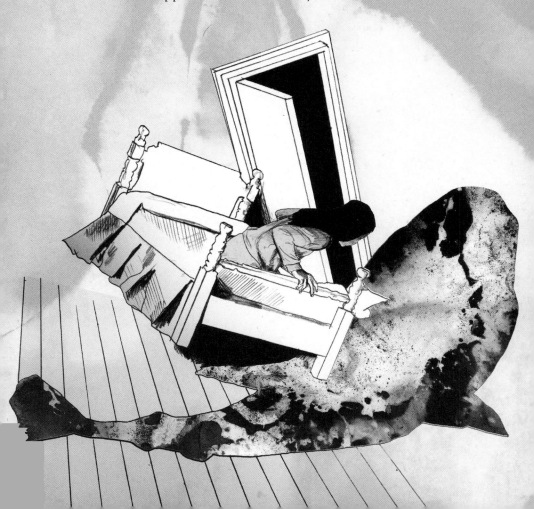

The bed was a boat,
the shark a tide,
and it pulled me so far out to sea
I was only a speck, a spot, a mote,
a dying star in an unending sky.

Eleven

Things at the lighthouse felt sticky and strange, like the air before a thunderstorm. Mum was lightning, sizzling with her unnatural energy, and Dad was the thunder, grumbling and rumbling and trying to talk her out of the boat. I don't know where Noodle and I fit in—I didn't feel like we did. All they talked about, snapped about, shouted about, was the boat, which was really about money. But Dad couldn't stop the boat coming.

Gin towed it to the little cove below the lighthouse in his old 4x4.

"You've got quite a project on your hands." He smiled. I was about to return it when I saw who was beside him. A sullen-faced, floppy-haired figure. Adrian. I shrank back in horror as he hopped out to help Dad unlatch the boat from the van.

Mum clapped her hands together.

"You'll see. It'll be the finest vessel Unst ever knew."

Gin chuckled, and Adrian laughed too, but it wasn't a nice laugh. I knew he wouldn't say anything with grown-ups there, but still I couldn't relax until Gin drove off, waving as they bumped away down the potholed road. We turned to look at the boat.

I could tell Dad was trying to put on a brave face for me, but I could also tell that he was worried. I was a little, too. Actually, I was a lot. Gin hadn't used it in years, and it was obvious why. It looked like a wreck, washed up on our rocky beach. The hull needed patching, and the stuffing on the benches in the small cabin was leaking out. The whole thing smelled of fish, and there was barely room for all the equipment Mum needed.

"It'll be snug," said Mum merrily, "but it's far speedier than *The Floe*. I'll chase down that shark in no time."

Kin came to help, and Mum put us in charge of tarring the hull. It made our hands black, and smelled of melting roads, and took days to fully fade off our skin. Dad went through the electronics. I got the feeling he was glad not to work on the lighthouse for a while. From the puffing and swearing that came from his office every day, and the fact that the lighthouse beam was still unlit, I wasn't sure it was going that well. He spent all week installing the software Mum needed, and drove to Mainland to buy new life jackets, flares, and distress beacons.

Before he left, Mum told him Gin was coming to check our work on the hull while he was at the shops, but he never showed up. When Dad came back and asked how it went, Mum said "Fine!" in that dazzlebright voice, and I chewed my tongue.

She rattled around the house, cooking big bean stews and planting chilis, replanting her tomato noodle pots and eating a lot of sausage rolls. She seemed distracted and absolutely focused all at the same time, and I wondered whether this was what Ms. Braimer meant when she said Mozart was a genius, but he was terrible at normal life.

Maybe her days and dreams were all full of the shark and its possibilities, like mine. But she couldn't be afraid of it like I was, or she wouldn't dare go out in an old boat to look for it.

Finally, a week after the rusting boat had arrived, it was ready for its maiden voyage.

"Looks good," said Dad, sounding impressed despite himself, and I agreed. Mum had painted it white and gray, like a seagull, and in great, looping, yellow letters she'd handwritten its name on the side, uneven and tailing off at a slant at the end where she'd got bored:

My heart swooped. Seeing my name like that, beside the shark's, made all Mum's moods worth it. I mattered, just as much as her research.

Dad towed it into the water, and we all cheered as no leaks came through. Kin and I high-fived.

"Excellent tarring," I said, bowing.

"And to you, good sir," he said, bowing back.

Mum snorted. "Very good indeed. We can invite Gin and his grandson out on it!"

Kin visibly flinched, but Mum rattled on. "Let's have a photo. I'll get the camera."

She went galloping inside, and Dad bent to pick up Noodle, an essential component of any photo our family takes.

"Well done us," he said, grinning at us both. "Maybe she'll be able to sell this on for a tidy profit in a few weeks."

My tummy went all swoopy then. I hadn't thought about how little time Mum had left to find the shark. Or how little time I had left with Kin. I didn't look at him, but he moved a bit closer, so maybe he was thinking the same thing.

A cry came from the lighthouse. Dad frowned but before he could move we saw Mum whirling down the slope, her oversized cardigan slipping down around her shoulders, her eyes wide.

"Did you do this?" she said, waving something at Dad. It was the camera, the spare one I'd taken star photos on.

"Mum?" She wheeled around, and tried to pull her cardigan back up. Kin took a step back.

"Julia, Kin, I think you should go inside for a minute." She turned back to Dad. "Did you borrow this?"

"No, Mum, I—" I swallowed. "I borrowed it. I kept it out of the rain . . ."

She pressed the button, and it whirred to life. The guilt retreated a little. It wasn't broken.

"Did you do this?" Her voice was calm, but shook a little at the edges. She was flicking through the pictures of the constellations.

"Yes—" I started.

"Did you delete some?"

"No, I—" I stopped, remembering the field, the swarm. "Maybe. It was full, the card. I checked they weren't of anything important."

"Weren't anything important," said Mum dully, and it was scarier than if she'd shouted. She turned to Dad helplessly. "Gretna Green, Dan. She deleted the photos I took at the murmuration, that last time."

It didn't mean anything to me, but it obviously did to Dad. "Maura, it's OK. You probably have them backed up somewhere."

But she was already shaking her head. "I lost the cable, remember? I was getting a new one sent. I never got round to it, with the funding stuff."

"Julia didn't know," said Dad. "It's OK, J. Isn't it, Mum?"

Mum's back was to me, and she was taking big, heaving breaths, like she was crying.

"Maura?" prompted Dad.

"Not now, Dan." Her voice broke. I knew it was my fault. My eyes smarted too, the lighthouse blurring behind her, the damp warping and spreading until it was all I could see. It was like the shark was bleeding through it, making everything shimmer and come loose.

"Why don't we . . ." said Dad, looking apologetically at Kin. "Kin, why don't we take a photo another time?"

I didn't want Kin to go, but I couldn't ask him to stay, not with Mum so clearly upset. A hot prickle of embarrassment scuttled across my cheeks and I ducked my head, feeling Kin look at me.

"It's fine," he said uncertainly. "I guess I'll go?"

The question in his voice was directed at me, but I didn't want to look up in case he saw the tears now dripping off my chin.

"I'll see you soon, Julia." I felt Kin's hand, warm and dry, squeeze mine briefly, and heard the crunch of Dad and Kin's shoes as they walked together up the slope to Kin's bike. When I was sure Kin was out of sight I looked up at Mum. She was hunched over the camera with her back to me, breathing deeply.

"Mum?"

She flinched, and I felt like I had when I fell off a jungle gym two years ago, all the air punched out of me.

Dad came back and pulled me into his warm side. "Mum, Julia needs a hug."

She turned, then. The camera was clutched to her chest, and her eyes were glassy as she looked at us. She looked like something from a sad film, the light seeming to settle gray and heavy over her shoulders, her skin mottled as the shark's.

"Mum?" Dad prompted. "Maura?"

Mum stepped forward and hugged me, but it felt spiky and strange, when normally Mum's hugs were like jumping into a warm bed. I couldn't hug her back, not properly.

"There," said Dad bracingly. "All better. Shall we take that photo, then?"

"Photo?" Mum let go of me, and was looking at the camera again. She seemed to have forgotten all about *Julia & the Shark*, bobbing in the shallows behind us.

Twelve

Mum went upstairs, and while Dad boiled the kettle I sat at the table with my insides churning like a washing machine in Kin's laundromat. Dad chattered cheerfully, and I could tell he was hoping I would forget what had just happened and be happy, but I couldn't.

"Dad," I said finally, when he stopped to draw breath. "What's Gretna Green?"

His shoulders tensed a little, but his voice was still light as he plopped the tea bag into the mug.

"Just somewhere important to your mum." I waited. Dad sighed. "A murmuration happens there."

"A murmuration." I turned the word over. It was familiar but I couldn't remember why.

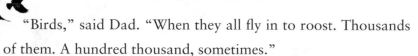

"Birds," said Dad. "When they all fly in to roost. Thousands of them. A hundred thousand, sometimes."

If I'd asked Mum, it'd have been a far more vivid description. But words are Mum's thing—trust Dad to have focused on the numbers.

"She scattered her mum's ashes there," he continued. "At the murmuration the year she was pregnant with you." I must have looked stricken, because Dad hurried on. "Don't worry. She's just tired. You know she's a monster when she's tired. This boat stuff has taken it out of all of us."

"But . . ." I bit my lip. I didn't know how to put what I wanted to say, and for the first time I wished I could think like Dad, put down my thoughts into a sum, express myself with an equation that he could easily understand.

"It's OK, Julia," said Dad softly. He was looking at me with very kind eyes, and it made me want to cry. "What is it?"

"I think I remember . . ."

Dad waited. I spoke to my lap, my fingers twisting white. I knew I had to say it like he would, binary and straight.

"She's been like this before."

Dad's listening became loud, you know how that happens when someone is really concentrating and you can feel the white noise of their attention.

I screwed up my eyes, the better to see the memory. Mum in the garden in Cornwall, scrunched up like a piece of old paper below the ash tree. Her shoulders shaking, the sound of her weeping. I shuddered, and looked up at Dad. His face was open and kind.

"I remember when I was little. She was walking around all strange and then she was crying in the garden."

Dad's touch landed lightly on my head, like he was trying to stop my racing thoughts. "You have such a clever brain, Julia. You were tiny when that happened."

"So it did happen?"

"Yes." Dad's voice was nearly a whisper. "When you were three. And another time, when she was pregnant. But it's nothing to do with you, Julia. It's the shark."

I hadn't thought it was until he said it. But the shark hadn't been there when she was pregnant, or when I was three. I had been. Now my heart began to beat very hard.

"She was fine then, and she'll be fine now," said Dad, seemingly taking my silence as a good sign, because he took his hand off my head. It felt like it was going to spin off my neck and float away. Dad strained the tea bag, placing it on the side so Mum could use the grounds for her tomatoes, and sloshed some milk into her favorite blue mug. "You want to take this up?"

Feeling oddly nervous, I circled the steps, the washing machine in my belly kicking up to its final crazed cycle. Their bedroom door was closed, Noodle sitting hopefully outside. Scratching her neck, I pressed my ear to the door, but if Mum was crying, I couldn't hear it. I knocked. There was no answer, and for a minute I thought about putting the tea down for Noodle and leaving. But that was stupid. It was only Mum.

I pushed open the door, Noodle snaking in behind me. The room was dim and airless, and a shape shifted on the messy bed. For a moment it looked like a deep sea, a fin breaking the waves—but then it was only Mum's hand as she reached out to me. "Come here, J."

Setting the tea down on the bedside table, I climbed in beside her. She was barely warm though the blankets were pulled right up to her chin, and her breath smelled sour. Still I snuggled in close, trying to get comfy next to the new, unfamiliar angles of her body. Noodle climbed on top of us both, stretching out like a sausage.

I tried to relax, to enjoy being with her. But her voice was too sad, her body too thin. She felt like a different person. She didn't even smell like Mum—she smelled of indoors. But soon, I reminded myself, she'd be out on the boat, and she'd go back to normal. She'd be fine, like Dad said she'd been before. She had to be.

We listened to Noodle purring. There was something that was nibbling at me, like those parasites that attach themselves to the Greenland shark's eyeball until it goes blind, and in the dark I felt all right to ask it.

"Mum? Why did you lie to Dad?"

Mum stiffened slightly, and Noodle let out a warning mew. "When?"

"About the hull, about getting Gin to come and check it?"

"Oh that." She relaxed again, yawning though it was only the afternoon. "Because Gin couldn't come for a while, and I wanted to get going. It was fine anyway, wasn't it?"

"You don't know that yet," I pointed out. The boat had only just gone in the water.

"I do know," she said, and it was so nice to hear her definite again I let it go.

"Why did you react like that, when I mentioned Gin's grandson?" She'd done that thing again, the leap from one thought to another without showing how she'd got there.

"Like what?"

"You want to talk about it?"

I shook my head, but she pushed on anyway. "My best friend got bullied at school. She had big ears, and one of the older boys used to lift her up by them."

"It's not that," I said, horrified. Kin had normal-sized ears, anyway. "Was she OK?"

"Oh yes," snorted Mum. "The thing about bullies is they pick on people who they think are weaker. So we worked out *his* weakness. He was scared of spiders, and I collected any dead ones I found for a week, and then put them down his shirt."

She mimed flailing about and screaming. Noodle jumped huffily off the bed and soon we were both laughing. Mum stopped first, and sighed. I could feel the atmosphere in the room shift again, becoming low and gloomy.

"It's going to be all right," said Mum, more to herself than to me. "I'm going to find the shark. I just need people to believe in me."

There was a horrible, plummeting sensation in my tummy. I hadn't believed in her lately. My yellow notebook, with its lines of crosses and coordinates, was proof. I'd become like Dad, looking at the numbers. I needed to be more like Mum. I used my words.

"I believe in you."

Mum laughed, but it was a hard sound, like a fist hitting wood. "Do you have fifteen million pounds, J?" Mum shifted impatiently. "Scooch over. You're squashing me."

Her eyes were starting to flutter closed, and I slid out of bed and pulled the door shut. But more than anything, it felt like Mum was shutting the door on me.

For once I was above water.
For once I wasn't afraid.
The sky stretched huge over me,
and at its height was a small flock of birds.

They dived and twisted and lifted, and as
they wove through the clear sky,
more joined them,
and more and more.

They were like a cloud now, a gathering
storm. And then there were so many the
sky started to crack at its edges, a blue
balloon swarmed by birds.

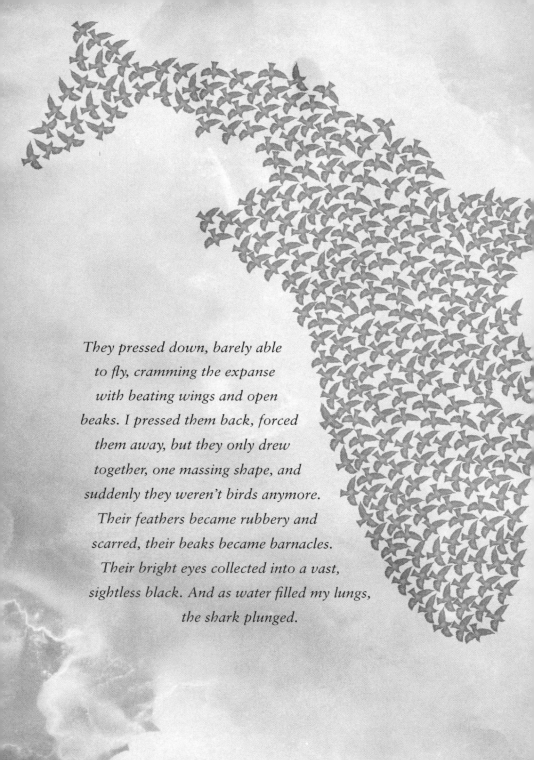

They pressed down, barely able
to fly, cramming the expanse
with beating wings and open
beaks. I pressed them back, forced
them away, but they only drew
together, one massing shape, and
suddenly they weren't birds anymore.
Their feathers became rubbery and
scarred, their beaks became barnacles.
Their bright eyes collected into a vast,
sightless black. And as water filled my lungs,
the shark plunged.

Thirteen

It was just the four of us on the maiden voyage of *Julia & the Shark*. Noodle liked the boat instantly, leaping onto the prow and leaning into the wind like a figurehead, which I took as a good sign. Another good sign was that when Mum let me turn the key in the ignition, the engine started on the first try.

"High-five, J!" she said.

She was trying, I could feel it. But that was part of the problem. Her smile seemed thin and fragile, like a tracing paper mask with the real frown showing through.

I sat down on the repaired leather seat, and Dad put his arm around me. I wondered if he noticed Mum's mask, too. His grip tightened when Mum started to steer the boat out of the bay,

sitting down heavily and closing his eyes. He didn't really like boats, which was a grave error when marrying Mum.

The lighthouse was soon a speck. The boat was fast, and even Mum slowed it a little, spray misting down over us, and soon my sweater was covered in a layer of neat droplets. I huddled deeper into Dad, and once we were on open sea, he seemed to relax a bit. The water was calm, with no wind making waves, and he moved to sit in the stern with Noodle on his lap.

Mum stopped the engine and brought over her nautical map to show me. It's laminated and massive. Fully open it would fill the whole of the lighthouse's kitchen, so it was folded into squares, covered in Mum's messy black writing. There were crosses dappled all over, and with a jab of guilt I remembered my notebook, all the marks I'd made highlighting Mum's daily failures.

"So here's where the shark was sighted last, by a fishing boat." She pointed to a place closer to Shetland than I'd expected. "And it only moves about half a mile an hour. So this is the radius I'll be exploring." She showed me the area—two squares' worth. Even though it looked small on the map, I knew a parcel of sea that big was not going to be easy to cover. Not when there was just one of her, and one of the shark.

"I can help," I said. "Come with you?"

"I don't think so," said Mum. "It'll be a squeeze with all my equipment." I tried to seem like it didn't hurt, but Mum wasn't even looking at me anyway.

I was as much worried as disappointed. The sea seemed very big out here. In Cornwall you could always see land, and I knew that in every direction there was either Ireland, or England, or Wales. But here there was nothing, our lighthouse a speck on

Unst, which was in turn a speck on the horizon behind us, so small and faint I felt like I could rub it from sight with my thumb. And Norway was somewhere over there, to the east, and Iceland to the west, and they felt like much wilder, far-off places than Mum was used to.

And somewhere in the depths was the shark, moving slower than time, growing more ancient and as steadily as a tree.

It was like the voyage of *Julia & the Shark* was a good omen, because the next day Dad finished his programming. He and Mum drank a whole bottle of wine each to celebrate, and we went outside to watch the lighthouse lighting itself automatically as soon as darkness fell. It stopped Kin and I stargazing from there, but sometimes he'd come to sit with me anyway, watching the beam sweep the sea, searching for something.

Some nights, Mum was out there too, and Dad woke with big rings like bruises under his eyes, and I barely slept. I distracted myself with the stars. There was a meteor shower due, and Kin and I had plans to go to the cliff nearby to watch, now that the light was working.

Though Dad was finished, there was no talk of us leaving early. I noticed Dad making phone calls to the bank back in Cornwall, and we had cupboard risotto most nights. Part of me insisted I didn't care, that anything was worth Mum finding the shark, but another quieter and larger part wished she would stop, and come back to me from the sea.

The night of the meteor shower, I got permission to meet Kin alone on the cliff because I said Neeta was going to be there too, but of course she wasn't. We cycled the ridge of the coast, the ground rising and the sky over us getting darker all the time as we left the lit lighthouse behind.

Kin had the telescope strapped to his back, and the bike light Dad made me use glinted off the metalwork. As we approached the spot Kin had shown me on the map, I smelled something. Smoke. Kin came to an abrupt halt, and I swerved to avoid hitting him.

"What?"

His eyes were huge under his helmet, and he was looking straight ahead. "Adrian," he mouthed.

I followed his gaze, and saw a small fire on the clifftop. Around it were three dark figures. I recognized the floppy hair straight away.

"We should go back," muttered Kin, making to turn his bike.

"No way," I said. "We've been looking forward to this all week. We can just go further on."

But Kin was shaking his head, and I was about to give up and follow him when a shout came from the fire.

"Flower! Whale!" I saw their silhouettes grow taller as the three of them stood and started towards us.

"Go!" said Kin in a panic, but he was unbalanced because of his telescope, sliding sideways off the seat and his pant legs catching in the gears.

I checked over my shoulder, thinking too late to turn off my bike light. The boys closed in as I helped Kin untangle himself.

"What have we here?" Adrian was smiling, his arms crossed, horribly lit by my bike light and flanked by his two friends. They looked like something from a horror movie. "Richard, Olly, look what we've found."

"Technically, we found you," I said.

"Technically," mimicked Adrian, and Richard and Olly laughed. "All right nerd, calm down."

"I am calm."

"So you are a nerd then?"

"Fine by me," I said. Kin was tugging on my sleeve, but I stood my ground. Mum had told me bullies reacted to weakness, so I would be strong. "I have a brain, at least."

Richard snorted, and Adrian elbowed him in the ribs. "Do whales even have brains?"

"Of course," I said, feeling bolder. "Way bigger than yours. Are you stupid or something?"

Olly snorted too this time, and Adrian rounded on him. "Cut it out."

"Julia, let's go," muttered Kin.

"What's that, Flower?" Adrian was now advancing on Kin, pointing at the telescope. "Give it here."

Kin backed away, his bike between his legs. "It's my dad's."

"He won't mind me having it. Give it here."

Adrian lunged for it, and Kin backed away, going sprawling. I heard an ominous *crunch* as he landed on the ground.

"Whoops," said Adrian in mock horror, as I hurried to help Kin up.

"If you broke it," I hissed furiously, glaring at the boy. I felt hatred running through me, pure and hot and powerful.

"I'll explain to his dad, shall I?" Adrian sounded bored. "Oh, but can he even understand English?"

This time it was me holding Kin back, and I had a lot more luck, being bigger than him.

"I'm going to tell your granddad what you said," I said. "He won't like it."

"See if I care," said Adrian. "How's your mum's boat, by the way? Has it sunk yet?"

Terror and rage sloshed in my stomach. I let go of Kin and stepped towards Adrian, my fingernails biting into my palms. "Don't say that."

"She's a weirdo, like you," said Adrian, grinning.

"So is your mum a loser like you?"

Adrian stopped smiling. "What did you say?"

"Where is she, even?"

Kin tugged my sleeve. "Julia—"

"Why isn't she around?"

"Shut up." Adrian's voice was low and threatening, but there was something else in it. Something shaking. A weakness, just like Mum said. I needled at it.

"Did she decide she didn't like you, and run away?"

"Take that back!" Adrian shouted.

"To be fair it must be disappointing." I felt powerful, staring at him on the cliff in the dark, his face very pale, his eyelid fluttering. I pulled the thread further out. "To have such a loser for a son."

Adrian unraveled.

I don't remember him hitting me. All I remember is being on the damp grass, the wind gone from my lungs, hands pulling Adrian away from me.

"You take it back!" he shouted, and there was a definite catch in his voice. As I lay gasping I saw his eyes were bright with tears.

"Leave it, Adrian." Richard and Olly pulled him away. "Let's go."

They ran off, pulling Adrian with them, back towards the fire. Kin dropped to his knees beside me. "Are you all right?"

I sat up slowly, experimentally rubbing my belly. "Yes. He just caught me by surprise."

"Not as much as you caught him." Kin's eyes were owl-huge. "How did you know?"

"Know what?"

"That stuff about his mum? It wasn't . . ." He hesitated. "It wasn't nice, Julia."

"He wasn't being nice," I said, amazed he seemed to be telling me off. "He asked if Mum's boat had sunk!"

"But it hasn't," said Kin. "And Adrian's mum *did* leave him. And his dad. A couple of years ago, in Year Four."

"I didn't know."

"Still," said Kin. He was looking at me like I was a stranger. "His dad wasn't a nice man. He used to talk to my dad the way Adrian talks to me, but way worse. He left too, last year. Went to work on an oil rig. That's why Adrian lives with Gin."

I struggled to my feet, remembering Adrian's face, the tears on his cheeks. I'd found his weakness, and now I felt slightly sick. Kin was inspecting the telescope.

"Is it all right?"

He shook his head, miserably. "I need to get it to Bapi."

I dusted off my jeans. "I'll come and explain."

"No," said Kin, a bit too loud. "You've done enough damage."

He cycled away, fading fast into the dark. His words seemed to echo in the night around me. Biting my lip to keep it from wobbling, I clambered back onto my bike, the thready light picking out the path back to the lighthouse.

As I got closer, I realized it was getting darker around me, not brighter. The light was out again, the outline of the lighthouse illuminated only by the stars. I put my bike back in the shed and went inside. Dad's voice drifted down swearily, Mum soothing him, and only Noodle came to greet me. I picked her up and started climbing the stairs. As I passed Dad's office, Mum poked her head out.

"Sorry about the language," she said. "We might have to give your dad a free pass on the swear jar. The light's stopped working."

"Yes, I think she might have noticed that," muttered Dad. I could see him up a ladder at the center of the room, red and green wires trailing like veins down his arms.

Mum rolled her eyes. "How was the meteor shower?"

"Kin couldn't make it," I lied. "I was just about to go and look."

"Lovely!" said Mum brightly, too distracted to even tell I was lying. "I'll come up in a bit. Take the crab net. We can try to catch some."

It was a silly joke, something I used to do as a child, trying to net stars in rock pools. But I fetched the net anyway, went to the platform, and waited.

126

Noodle got bored and leapt out of my arms, slinking back inside. I waited a bit longer, and the sky started to spark. Bright points of light began to streak across the sky, one or two at first,

and then one or two a minute. I picked up the crab net, waving it over the railing, imagining a hot white piece of starlight landing in it. It would burn right through.

Suddenly, a flare of light came from behind me. I heard a small cheer as the beam began its slow blink. I looked out at the sea, so vast, the stars so far away, and my arms reaching out my tiny crab net.

"Stupid," I muttered, dropping the net. I wrapped my arms around my knees, wishing Kin was there to tell me what I was seeing, wishing I could stop thinking of Adrian's stupid, tear-streaked face, wishing I could stop the hot cauldron of guilt churning in my stomach.

As the stars seemed to fall from the sky,

and Mum still didn't come,

I'd never felt more alone.

The walls were moving. They bulged, and pulsed, mold chasing itself up the walls until it was dark, dark as the ocean. The shark stirred, enormous, slow, unstoppable. The floorboards creaked as it shunted against them, pressing its bulk until they splintered and the whole bed rose, the lighthouse ripped from its roots, as the shark surfaced and carried us all out to sea.

Fourteen

Things got worse the next day. When I came down for breakfast in the morning, Mum and Dad were sitting at the kitchen table, looking at me sternly.

"Sit down, Julia," said Mum. "Gin's just called. Adrian came home in tears last night. He said you teased him about his mother leaving."

Dad's forehead creased. "Julia, how could you?"

"I didn't know. I didn't!" I said, as Dad raised his eyebrows in disbelief. "I just guessed, because he lives with Gin."

"Why would you do that?" Dad asked.

"He was bullying Kin. He's horrid."

"You should have told a grown-up."

"I did, sort of. Mum told me what to do."

"What?" Mum looked confused.

"You told me about your friend, and finding a bully's weakness, and I thought—"

Dad made a furious sound, like an enraged bull. "All right, Julia. Go upstairs. I want you to write a letter to this boy, to apologize."

"But—"

"No buts. One of us has to teach you right from wrong—"

"Excuse me—" started Mum, but Dad continued talking to me.

"Go. I want to read it before you send it."

In a silly song we sing at school assemblies, it said that rainbows always follow rain. But that day, that week, it felt like the rain never stopped. Not only did I have to write that letter to Adrian, but Dad said I was grounded. Not that I had anywhere to go, with Kin so angry.

The worst part was Mum. One day, Dad had to go to Mainland to get a new screwdriver, and she had to stay and look after me even though the day was still and calm, perfect for the boat.

"I'm running out of time," she said. I could hear her foot tapping the kitchen tiles, while I hid up the staircase with my book as an alibi, listening. "Can't you take her?"

"I think she'd rather have a day with her mum," said Dad. "Why don't you take her out on the boat?"

"I told you," snapped Mum. "There's no room. She'll get in the way."

My stomach plunged through the step below me. I knew I was irritating Mum recently, but I didn't know how much until that moment.

"Not to look for that shark," hissed Dad. "To spend *time* with her, Maura."

"But I don't *have* time!" Mum's voice burst from the kitchen, and I had already heard enough. I climbed to the beam, heaving my heavy heart with me.

Dad drove off a short while later, and Mum didn't even come looking for me until lunch. I watched the sea, and reread my book that I dreaded having to return to the laundromat, and saw the postman come and go before she called up the spiral staircase.

Mopily, I flopped down onto a kitchen chair, while Mum cut thick slices off the loaf of bread Dad had baked that morning, sending steam into the kitchen. It was too hot, the wood burner piled up high and roaring, but Mum didn't seem to notice, even when her glasses steamed up.

Searching for something to say, my eyes landed on a thin envelope on the table. It was addressed to Mum, and had a university logo stamped into one corner. It couldn't be good news, or Mum would have told me, would have come dancing up the stairs, a big smile on her face. Instead, I could see her face was red and raw-looking under its tan, her lips pulled thin as the envelope.

"Mum . . ." I started, but I didn't know what to say. She didn't hear me anyway, busy opening a can of tomato soup and pouring it into the pan. As she waited for it to heat, she stood looking out of the window, which was too fogged for her to see anything.

I pretended to read my book, about Greek gods arriving into modern life to help a boy with his sick mum, but really I was watching her. She was as inscrutable as the window, the shadows under her eyes the same color as the mold on the wall behind her. It seemed to bulge in the too-hot kitchen, blossoming before my eyes, ballooning like Adrian's neck, like something was breathing in the walls.

Mum poured the soup into two bowls, and buttered my bread for me.

"We can go in the boat tomorrow," she said suddenly. "Maybe we can find those famous otters."

"What? I mean, yes," I said, confused but seizing on the idea. "I'd like that."

She rambled on about otters, about how their fur is so thick their skin never gets wet, how they use tools like rocks to open shells, and I pretended to be noting them in my notebook, but all the while I was watching her. Her eyes seemed to get further and further away, as though she was being carried on the tide of her own voice, out to sea.

When we were finished, Mum washed up, taking the empty tomato soup can and rinsing it in the sink, staring out of the window again. I watched her as she soaped it, red running down the enamel.

"Mum," I said, scrambling over to her. "Your finger."

She looked down, dazed. Her finger was bleeding where she'd cut it on the can.

"Yuck," she said, swaying. "Sorry, Julia."

"You don't need to say sorry, Mum. Do you need a bandage?"

"I'll get it." She tottered again, walking up the stairs heavily, like she was a hundred years old. I waited for her to come down again, but she didn't. I went up, and found her in her and Dad's bedroom, still in her clothes and asleep, curled like a question mark on their sheets.

Dad got home just after six. He was whistling tunelessly, carrying a tote bag of shopping, and smiled broadly when I opened the door for him.

"Perfect timing, J-cat. Did you go out on the boat?"

"No, but Mum said we can look for otters tomorrow. Dad—"

"Brilliant!" He put the kettle on the stove. "I'll come with you. I love otters. When I was young—"

"Dad."

"What's wrong?" He looked around the kitchen, at the washed-up bowls and the envelope in the center of the table. He sighed heavily, and set down the tote bag. "That's that then." He smiled at me sadly. "Is she all right?"

"I don't think so. She's in bed."

"It's OK, J. She tried, and that's what matters. It's a shame, but maybe now she can do something else."

"She doesn't want to," I said. "She wants to find the shark."

He began unpacking the shopping. "I think she needs a rest now, don't you?"

"I guess. But she never stays in bed all day. Is she really sick?" I could tell Dad wasn't saying something, and I pushed on. "Is it what Grandma had?"

Dad stopped unpacking. "What makes you say that?"

"Mum said Grandma was in bed all the time before . . . before she . . ."

Dad took my hand. "Your grandma had dementia."

"Yes, but before that, was she like Mum?"

"It's all right. Mum's just very tired."

"She's never like this," I insisted.

Dad hesitated, and ran his thumb along his jaw, the way he does when he's searching for words. I could tell he wished it was something he could explain in numbers. "Mum is brilliant, yes? Her brain is brilliant. It's also complicated, and sometimes, things go wrong. Sometimes she feels happy, but it's almost too happy. Like that day with the boat, remember?" I nodded, recalling the flowers, the wine, Mum's too-bright smile. "So then the opposite happens. She gets sad."

"Is that why she's in bed?"

"I think so," said Dad. "This research has really got to her, the rejection, I mean. She's worked too hard, and her brain's got tired."

I nodded, taking it all in. It made sense, in a strange way, why Mum sometimes bounced around like Tigger, and other times she was mopey like Eeyore. "But she'll be all right?"

"Of course," said Dad bracingly. "These things just take time. When we're home she can take it easier. You don't have to worry about anything, Julia."

But he was wrong.

I had to worry about everything.

The shark was back.

It carried the
lighthouse out to
sea, further each time,
to a place of ice floes,
the world locked together
by cold. Its skin was rough as
bark, my whole room papered
with it, and it was living rock,
a fossil with crystals shining deep
inside its eyes. Sightless, it turned for the
fathomless deep.
I knew Mum was beside me,
still as stone, but I couldn't
reach her, couldn't see her
and even though I called, she
didn't answer before the
shark
slid under
the ice,
carrying us
all deeper under.

Fifteen

"Julia." Dad shook me gently. "Sorry, Julia. It's all right."

"What?" I sat up blearily, and Dad turned my bedside light on. I squinted at him. My clock said ten past midnight, but he was fully dressed with a coat and gloves, his boots unlaced and trailing mud across the floor. "Have you been outside?"

"I need you to get up," he said, and though his voice was calm the room crackled with tension. "Everything's all right, but I need you to get dressed. I'm going to drop you at Mr. Ginley's house. I tried to get him to come here, but his grandson's at home."

"Adrian? I can't go there."

"It's all right," he repeated. "He's not angry at you."

The more he said everything was all right, the more I realized something was very wrong. "Why?"

"I need to take your mum somewhere. She'll be OK, but it can't wait until morning."

I looked down at his boots, the laces untied. "Where have you been?"

"Come on."

I was too confused to ask the right questions. I got up dumbly, and dressed in a mismatch of clothes, picking up my notebook and following him downstairs. Noodle was meowing and rubbing at our ankles.

"Can I take her?"

"We'll be back soon," he said. "Mr. Ginley's grandson is allergic."

Of course he is, I thought bitterly, bending to rub Noodle's ears.

"I've filled her bowl. Please, Julia," said Dad. "There's no time."

It was really serious, then. There was always time to stroke Noodle and check she was settled before we went anywhere, even for a night. I looked at the coat hook. Mum's coat was still hanging there.

"Dad," I said, properly frightened now. "Where's Mum?"

"Somewhere safe," said Dad. "Please, Julia, I have to get back."

"Get back where?"

But he was already striding off down the driveway to the car, and I hesitated only a moment longer before snatching Mum's raincoat from the hook and tripping after him, pulling the door shut behind me.

Mr. Ginley lived above his shop. The apartment was warm and filled with shells on every surface like my bedroom at home, and smelled of tobacco and kippers, which was a lot nicer than it sounds. Adrian wasn't up when I arrived, which I was glad about, seeing as I looked like I'd dressed in the dark, which of course I had.

"Thanks for doing this, Mr. Ginley," said Dad. "It'll only be for tonight. I'll pick her up in the morning."

"Not at all," said Gin in his rumbling, kind voice. "My Mary had her share of troubles. I understand. She'll be all right with me."

Dad hugged me, and ran back out into the rain. With a jolt, I realized he'd left the car running. He never did this, ever, because of the environment. He and Mum would even go up to people in the school pickup line in Cornwall and tell them to turn off their engines because of the emissions. It really was an emergency, bigger than climate change.

Gin had made up a bed on the sofa, with a little plug-in night-light that projected dolphins on the walls. "That's Adrian's favorite." He winked. "He won't be happy if he knows I've nicked it."

I stored this information to share with Kin, then remembered we weren't friends at the moment. I felt a bit sick, knowing Adrian was nearby. "Is he . . ."

"Asleep. And you mustn't worry about all that business at the cliff. I try to keep an eye on him, but with his parents gone . . ." he trailed off. "I hope he'll come round. Not like his father."

"What's happening?" I asked tentatively. "Is my mum all right?"

"She's in the best place. Here, I made you a hot chocolate. I'm just in my study," he said, pointing at an open door. I couldn't see a bed in the tiny room, only an armchair with a blanket draped over it. "Adrian's got my bedroom. So if you need me, just knock."

He closed the door softly, and I lay down on the sofa. It was broad and quite saggy. I watched the dolphins leaping across the walls. Though I was sure I would never be able to sleep, my body dragged me down, and soon I felt the world melt away.

Groggily, I opened my eyes. Daylight was seeping in through the curtains, and Adrian was sitting at the kitchen table across the room from me, eyeing me suspiciously.

I sat up and tried to comb my hair flat.

"Morning," said Gin merrily, stirring a pot. "Porridge? I have salt in mine but Addie here likes strawberry jam."

I sat as far away from Adrian as possible, which wasn't very far considering the table was smaller even than the one at the lighthouse. Gin placed a bowl in front of me.

"Thank you." I blew on the steaming porridge. "Has my dad called?"

"He'll be round about ten. Sorry about the early start, I've got to open the shop soon and wanted to see you fed."

I nodded. I was desperate to ask about Mum, but I didn't want to in front of Adrian.

"Jam? Homemade," twinkled Gin.

I took it tentatively, and spooned in a glob.

"You stir it in." Adrian was watching me. He seemed to be trying to be nice. I stirred, and tasted. "Good?"

I nodded. I had to admit, it was great.

"Right," said Gin, checking his watch. "I need to open up. I think Addie has a few things to say. I'll be downstairs if you need anything."

He closed the door, and we heard his footsteps disappearing down the stairs. Adrian's eyes were determinedly fixed on his empty bowl.

"Sorry," he said. I blinked at him, astonished.

"What?"

"Sorry," he said, a little louder. "I am. I'm going to see Kin today too, to apologize. I've been an idiot."

I was too shocked to speak.

"It's not an excuse," he carried on, talking to his spoon. "But I was jealous, I guess."

"Of Kin?"

"And you." He shrugged. "Your parents. They really care about you."

A lump filled my throat. I wasn't sure, in that moment, if it was true.

"Anyway," said Adrian briskly. "I'm sorry, and I mean it. And sorry about your mum."

"What about her?"

"About the hospital."

My heart throbbed painfully. "What?"

He hesitated. "She's at the hospital. On Mainland."

I felt my mouth fall open. "The hospital? Why?"

Adrian looked aghast, paler than ever. "I thought you knew," he said. "I heard my granddad on the phone with your pa. She took some pills—"

"Pills?" It made no sense. "What do you mean?"

"I . . ." Adrian searched for the words in his bowl. "Nothing."

"Tell me," I said, desperation making my voice too loud, and he jumped.

"Julia—"

"Tell me!" I pushed my chair back from the table, and it caught on the rug, clattering to the floor. I stumbled towards Adrian, desperate for him to explain, and he leapt up, placing his own chair between us like a shield. I knew I was scaring him, but I didn't care.

"That's all I know, I swear!" said Adrian, cringing. "She took pills. You know. Lots of them."

A roaring sound started to fill my ears. I felt salt stinging my eyes, and my voice retreated to a whisper small as the sea caught in a shell. "She . . . she tried to . . ."

I couldn't voice it. Couldn't even think it. Not Mum. Not my mum, loud and lovely and brilliant. But she hadn't been lately, had she? Even her face had changed as she lost weight, even her smell. My hands started to shake, and I clenched them tightly.

"I don't know anymore, honest I don't. She had to go to the hospital."

"I have to go." My voice was drowned out by the roaring sound in my ears, like waves smashing a beach, my vision blotchy and blurred as sharkskin.

"No," said Adrian. "You should stay here. I'll get my granddad—"

"I want to go now." Salt was in my throat now too, like the sea was spilling out from inside me, filling me. The walls began to warp, like I was stuck in one of my dreams. The shark was here. The shark had found me.

"Sit down, Julia." Adrian's hand was gentle on my shoulder, but I pushed him away roughly.

"I want to go," I snarled, and Adrian raised his hands in surrender.

"You can take my bike," he said. "It's outside. If Granddad sees you—"

"He won't." Mum's raincoat was lying slack on the sofa, crumpled and empty. I shuddered as I put it on. Mum's spare lighthouse key was in the pocket, attached to the key for the boat, and I gripped it tight enough to hurt.

"Are you sure you don't want to stay? I could get Kin . . ."

But would Kin even come? He'd made it clear he hated me for what I'd said to Adrian, and everything was unraveling like the loose thread I'd pulled on the clifftop. But it was my life that was coming apart. I'd said Adrian's mum had left because of him, and now my mum—she had . . . she had tried to . . .

Was it me? Dad's voice came back, that day in the kitchen. *It was nothing to do with you, Julia.* But grown-ups lied, and what if Dad was lying now? The walls shuddered, the floorboards rolling as though I stood on a boat. The thought was too horrid to bear. There must be another explanation. My heart thudded. *The shark. The shark. The shark.*

"I really think you should stay," said Adrian nervously. He seemed scared to touch me. "You don't look well."

I shook my head, and breathed deeply to try to calm my heart, but it wouldn't stop hammering against my throat. I had to get out of this tiny room, away from Adrian. I wanted Mum, or Dad, but Noodle would have to do. Pulling the coat tight around me, I opened the creaky door and flew down the narrow staircase.

It spat me out in the far corner of the shop. The high, cluttered shelves shielded me from the counter where Gin was busy with a customer, and it was easy enough to slip past him. Adrian's bike was unlocked outside, as he'd said. Across the road, the door to the laundromat was closed, the windows fogged up. I longed to see Kin, for everything to be OK between us. When had everything gone so rotten? Heart swooping, I started to pedal.

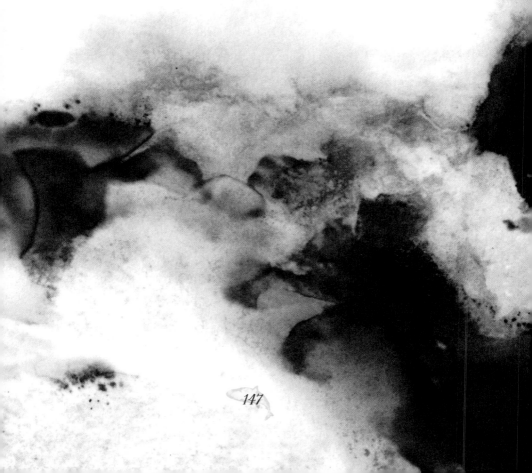

147

Sixteen

I knew Mum and Dad wouldn't be there, but still my heart sank when I turned the spare key in the rusty lock and pushed my way into the empty kitchen. Noodle wrapped herself around my ankles, mewling, and I paused long enough to fill her bowl with fresh food and water, careful to avoid looking at the mold on the walls. My hands were still shaking, my body still unsteady as I took the stairs two at a time.

I stopped outside their bedroom. I hadn't been inside since I'd left Mum curled on the sheets, and I hesitated, but Noodle had finished her meal. She came upstairs and nosed in through the gap, jumping onto the desk and rolling for a belly scratch. I went in after her, holding back tears as I looked around for clues, something to show what had happened to Mum, why she had done what she did.

"What do I do?" I murmured to Noodle, my voice breaking. She mewed and I walked over to the desk. It was papered in rejection letters, but something broke the monotonous black and white. A photo.

Mum was younger, in a blue floral dress, her hair loose, her arms cupping her swollen belly. Cupping me.

She was turning away from the camera, and her face was slightly blurred, but there was no mistaking her expression. She looked hollow-eyed with sadness, like she had the last few days, and I remembered Dad saying she had been miserable after her mum died, while she was pregnant with me. But she looked more than miserable. She looked sunken in, shrunken.

I shuddered, and buried the photo in the bottom of a drawer. As I turned it facedown, I saw something scrawled on the back in green ink.

Never Again

All the breath rushed out of me. Here it was, the proof I didn't want to find . . . did she mean having a baby?

Did she mean me?

Knock knock knock.

I ran down the stairs, scrabbling for the door. It would be Dad, maybe even Mum—

"Captain Bjorn?"

His hand was raised to knock again, and he lowered it.

"Julia," he said in his gentle voice. "Is your mother here?"

I remembered her talking about him not believing in her research, and glowered at him. "She's not."

"Ah. Will she be back soon?"

"No."

"That is rotten luck," he said, sighing. "Rotten luck. Is there any way of contacting her?"

"No." I narrowed my eyes. "Why?"

"The shark," he said, and my breath caught in my chest. "One's been sighted, not too far from here. Just below the surface, they think cruising for prey, possibly. I would go myself but I'm about to sail for Oban." He held out a piece of paper. "I wrote down the coordinates. It'll have moved on by now, but not far. It moves slow—"

"Half a mile an hour," I said shakily.

He nodded. "Exactly. If she can leave in the next hour, she'll have a good chance of catching it tonight."

I took the paper in trembling fingers. Captain Bjorn smiled at me, and made to leave, before turning back.

"Can you also tell her sorry?" He grinned ruefully. "I was skeptical at first, of course, but . . . it's a shame the universities were not funding her. If I could have worked any longer for free, I would have. But I have my crew, and it is not only my family who have to eat."

My whole body was trembling. My ears were full of water, the floor unsteady. Captain Bjorn frowned. "You are not here on your own?"

"No," I lied. "My dad's upstairs."

"Perhaps I could speak to him?"

"He's working," I said hurriedly. "He can't be disturbed."

"All right," said Captain Bjorn. "Well, I wish you luck, Miss Julia. I hope me and your mum will make friends again, and I can come back for dinner soon. That cupboard risotto was quite delicious."

He smiled warmly and left. I shut the door and unfolded the paper he'd given me.

I suddenly understood why Dad thought numbers were so beautiful. Here it was, the shark Mum had searched for all these weeks. I stroked the paper, and rummaged in Mum's coat pocket, drawing out the keys to *Julia & the Shark*.

The roaring in my ears stopped. The floor ceased rocking. My heartbeat became more like a drum, like a battle thrum. I imagined the shark moving below me, slower than time. It had followed me onto land, and now I would chase it back to the sea. I would find it, for Mum. I would show her I believed in her when no one else did. I could make it all better, could make Mum proud, make her happy she had me. I knew what I had to do.

Seventeen

Julia & the Shark sat high in the water, bobbing gently like a gull. I waded out to her, Noodle in my arms, and climbed on, hauling her anchor into the stern. Something like hope filled my chest as I drew out the coordinates Captain Bjorn had written down.

63°30'31.7"N 02°917.1"W

Clipping them onto the clipboard beside the huge folded map, I keyed them into the navigation system with great care. Every digit was important, and if I got just one wrong, I would end up miles off course.

The headboard blinked into life, and Noodle jumped onto

the padded bench, purring contentedly. For a moment I felt overwhelmed, all the lights blinking on and off, compass spinning, radar beeping, but then I took three deep breaths, just like Mum had taught me.

"Most of these don't matter," she'd said. "You just need to know this. That means go, that means stop. That means turn. That means help."

I turned the wheel, aiming the boat out of the bay, and sailed into open sea. I didn't look back for ages, eyes fixed to the ever-vanishing horizon. After about an hour, the radio crackled to life.

"*Julia & the Shark*, this is the harbor master. Please confirm your destination, over." I scrambled to pick it up, deepening my voice as I pressed the *transmit* button and spoke as I'd heard Mum do.

"Hello, harbor master, this is *Julia & the Shark*."

"What is your destination?"

I hesitated. "Oban."

"Please be advised, heavy sou'westerly with increased pressure zone coming. Advise you return to harbor."

Knowing I was going nowhere near Oban, I dismissed the worry before it started.

"Negative," I said, trying to sound like the submariners in Dad's favorite film. "We are confident of our course."

"Noted," said the harbor master. "Safe sailing."

"Roger," I said, wincing at the chuckle on the other end.

"It's Pete, actually," said the voice. "Keep the radio on."

The boat moved fast on the flat water, cutting a frothy trail behind us that soon melted into nothing. When I finally glanced over my shoulder, land was gone. Only the sea for miles.

The summer days were long this far north, and I was only going further in that direction, towards the Arctic. Captain Bjorn had said Mum could reach the shark by evening, and so could I.

Our supplies were limited to a very brown, very soft banana and an equally soft orange I'd found in the fruit bowl, and a couple of tins of sardines in oil from the cupboard. Thanks to Mum and Dad not having a telly back home in Cornwall, I was used to being bored, and it's actually quite hard to feel bored when you're on your own with a cat in the middle of the sea.

My mind kept circling back to Mum, cutting through the surface of every other thought like a fin, and I wrestled it back down each time. If I could find the shark, and tell her so, then she would be all right. She would be happy again. She would be Mum again.

Even rescuers get hungry. The porridge had been a good idea, and my tummy didn't start to rumble until the clock on the boat's dashboard flicked over to three in the afternoon. Noodle started to meow around then too, her fur on end to keep her warm. It was matted with salt and sticky to the touch.

We had been at sea for over six hours. Dad would have come to Gin's at ten, would have checked the lighthouse. Perhaps, I realized too late, I should have left a note. But there hadn't been enough time. There were still hours to go until I reached the shark. Guilt tangled in my mind, but I brushed it away. Dad would be fine. It was Mum I needed to worry about.

My stomach grumbled again, so I checked the wheel was fixed on course, and sat on the padded seat, pulling the supplies towards us. I knew I should only eat a little, save the rest for later and our return trip, but suddenly the banana was gone, and the orange, and Noodle had licked the sardine tin clean. She meowed for more, so I shared the second tin with her, running my finger around the inside.

"We probably shouldn't have done that," I said to Noodle, but she only bent over and started licking her bum. I guess cats don't really care about rationing.

It was starting to get cold, though the sky was still light. I searched the cupboards under the seats, and found blankets for Noodle, the flares Dad had brought Mum when she bought the boat, and a whole tub of sausage rolls. I stored them gratefully, within reach of the wheel, and as I went to close the cupboard I spotted a blister pack of pills. It was empty, and my stomach flipped, remembering how Adrian had said *lots of them*. I kicked the packet into the dark back of the cupboard, and slammed the door shut.

Noodle burrowed into the blanket, turning so only her pink nose showed from the musty fabric. I clamped my hand under my arm, letting the long sleeve of Mum's coat fall over the one on the wheel. I imagined I was her, as she used to be, brave and brilliant, and stopped trembling.

The hours dragged by, with only the sighting of seagulls and a couple of seals. I crossed my arms, and watched the blinking lights of the navigation system. The soft beeps of the radar were like a lullaby, the rocking waves soothing. I let my head tilt back, only for a moment.

The radio crackled, like tinfoil against my eardrums. I stumbled to my feet, tripping over the blanket, hearing Noodle mew.

"Noodle," I said admonishingly. "Why didn't you wake me?" Her eyes glowed back at me.

It was dark, properly nighttime, but there were no stars, only a thick blanket of cloud. I wished I could see Dhruva Tara, Polaris, the North Star, the lodestar.

I checked the time—11:39 p.m.—and our coordinates. *63°30'31.7"N 0°29'17.1"W.*

"We're here," I said, checking the map. "We're here!"

I shouted it, and my voice went on and faded into nothing. I swallowed, looking around. Nothing and nothing and nothing. I could have been alone in the world. I could have been in space.

My teeth started to chatter. The boat swayed, and it no longer felt like a cradle. I spoke into the silence, to try to fill it.

"Time to turn on the radar," I told Noodle. The radio crackled again, and I ignored it, focusing on twisting the knobs, checking the depth gauge. 500 meters. I swallowed. That was very deep water.

The waves were a little rougher now, rolling the boat around like a skipping stone. Far off, there was a flash, and a moment later, a rumble of thunder. That storm the harbor master had promised. But it was far away, and I would miss it by miles.

"We're all right," I said to Noodle. "We're all right."

She licked her paw, unconcerned, which calmed me a little, too.

The boat lights swung over the rolling waves. The boat was really rising and falling now, feet at a time, the hull slapping the water. I winced, wishing Mum had paid a professional to tar the hull, and not relied on Kin and me. Still, it had served her all right. The boat was sound. Dad wouldn't have let her out in it if it wasn't. But then again, he thought Gin had checked it, when I knew he hadn't.

Another flash, and I was sure it wasn't my imagination that it was closer this time. I heard no thunder, but the wind was louder, rushing in at my ears and grasping at Mum's coat, whipping its toggles against my face.

"I'm just going to put you down here," I said to Noodle, lifting her down to my feet, slotting her safely behind the pedals. She burrowed deeper under the blankets.

I tried to stop my hands shaking. *Julia & the Shark*'s light swept the sea, and the stars were still gone, swept up under the rug of clouds, thickening all the time over my head.

I shuddered. Sou'westerly, the harbor master had said. But maybe he'd made a mistake. Or maybe I hadn't heard him right, because the next flash of lightning was much, much closer, illuminating the endless, rolling sea, and not even the screaming wind could disguise the grumble of thunder, so loud I felt rather than heard it, rippling under the soles of my feet.

Suddenly the steadiness I'd felt since deciding to find the shark evaporated. What had I done? I'd brought Noodle out into the middle of the ocean, in search of a shark not even my mum could find.

Panic poured into the space where my certainty had been, hot and sharp. I should have stayed at Gin's. I should have waited for Dad and got my answers from him. A high sound grated my ears and I realized I was making a frightened squeak like a trapped fox, a horrible noise that frightened me more than the approaching storm. I closed my eyes. I couldn't lose control here. There was no way to wake up from this nightmare.

"We have to go," I said aloud, to make it real. "We have to go back."

Another lightning flash, burning my eyes, and Noodle yowled almost as loud as the thunder.

"All right," I said to her, kneeling down under the navigation board, pressing my body close to her. "I'll take us home. It's all right."

Groping for one of the flares, I sent it blazing into the sky.

The lightning whipped the sea, the waves climbed, and now the rain came. It didn't begin like usual, with a few drops giving warning. It was like someone emptied a mighty bucket over the boat. Instantly I felt water slosh around my ankles.

I lifted Noodle again, wedging her into the cupboard next to Mum's sausage rolls.

I used one of the empty tubs to bail out some of the water, my fingers instantly freezing, but it was pointless. I skidded on the slick floor and hit my head on the padded seat, my temple slapping against the hard plastic beneath. Dazed, I dropped the empty bucket, and it bobbed on the sloshing water. My feet were numb, my shoes soaked through, and my head felt hot. There was no point bailing. Our best hope was trying to outrun it.

Reaching for the wheel, I readied to spin it, when the radar beeped. I froze, the wind stinging my face, and watched the screen.

Something huge was moving. Something massive, only meters from the boat.

I hit the side, hands slick on the guardrail. The waves rocked me up and down, lifting me from my feet while I kept tight hold of the metal. I couldn't see anything. And then, in another flash of lightning, much too close, was a massive shape.

Just below the surface, a vast, pitted expanse.

It felt like the storm dropped, just for a moment. I swung the boat light around and saw greenish skin, the surface scarred and rough as seaweed. It was impossible, and real, and the smell hit my nostrils so hard it was like a slap. Something sharp and rotten and alive, animal and ancient.

The shark.

My hands loosed the light and it swung crazily away, dragging
a thick line across the surface and the shark did not seem to end,
it seemed to go on until the whole sea was shark, green and torn
by time. I could have sworn I saw an eye, black and glinting,
thick with crystals, rolling away from the boat light.
And then, slowly, so slowly,
it began to dive.

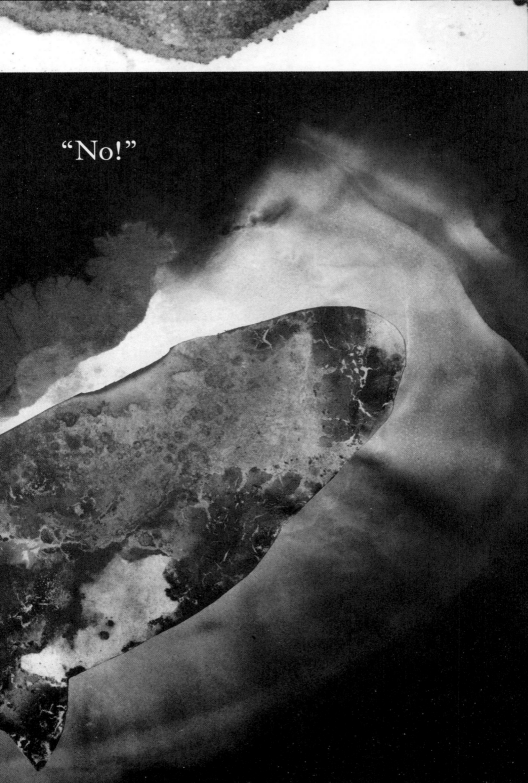

"No!"

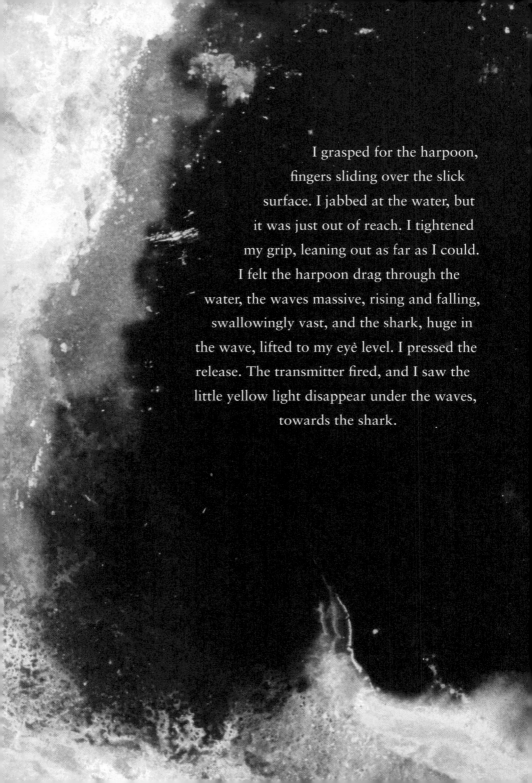

I grasped for the harpoon,
fingers sliding over the slick
surface. I jabbed at the water, but
it was just out of reach. I tightened
my grip, leaning out as far as I could.
I felt the harpoon drag through the
water, the waves massive, rising and falling,
swallowingly vast, and the shark, huge in
the wave, lifted to my eyè level. I pressed the
release. The transmitter fired, and I saw the
little yellow light disappear under the waves,
towards the shark.

The boat tipped, and just as my heart
leapt, I felt my gravity shift. The world spun
away from me, and suddenly I wasn't on the boat
anymore. My hand no longer held the guardrail.
My hand no longer held anything at all.
Something told me to take a breath, and I did, just
as the water closed over me like an icy fist, and the
waves knocked all the air from me.

I didn't feel anything.

The cold was too absolute, too consuming.

It was so cold, it was almost warm.

The pain in my temple vanished, and all was quiet,

the thunder a far-off purr.

I tried to kick, tried to move my arms,

but Mum's coat had slipped over my shoulders.

It was dragging me down.

It could only have been a moment,

but I felt like I was a whale, a tree, a shark, time

moving slower for me, as I felt the coat tighten,

holding me close as one of Mum's hugs.

It was easy to stop kicking,

much easier than forcing

my way to the surface.

The cold was a cloud,

as heavy as one, as wet and total,

and Mum's coat shrunk close

and sucked at me,

tugging

me

down.

Something nudged my legs.
They were so numb,
it felt like it was happening very far away.
A current, helping to pull me deeper?

*Feebly, I opened my stinging eyes, seeing light
like stars covering the whole world. It was so
cold. My legs were nudged again,
and this time I moved, a definite movement
up, some instinct knowing which way was
which even without air in my lungs to carry
me to the surface.*

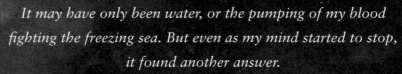

It may have only been water, or the pumping of my blood fighting the freezing sea. But even as my mind started to stop, it found another answer.

It was something rough and alive, something traveling since Mozart played, seen rarely enough to be myth. It was something blind and beautiful and terrifying, nosing its way through the dark, through history, through our lighthouse and my dreams. It was the answer to Mum's darkness, the thing that had led her there, and could lead her out of it. And now, it was here to do the same for me. And then there were lights in the water, real lights, and something slapped down on the surface. A ring, a halo, dark against the lights sweeping over.

Mum's coat was heavy as a pocketful of stones,
the rubber stuck to my frozen skin.

And though I did not want to,
though I wanted to hold onto the coat
like it was Mum, and haul it to the surface,
I let it slip over my shoulders.

I let it go.

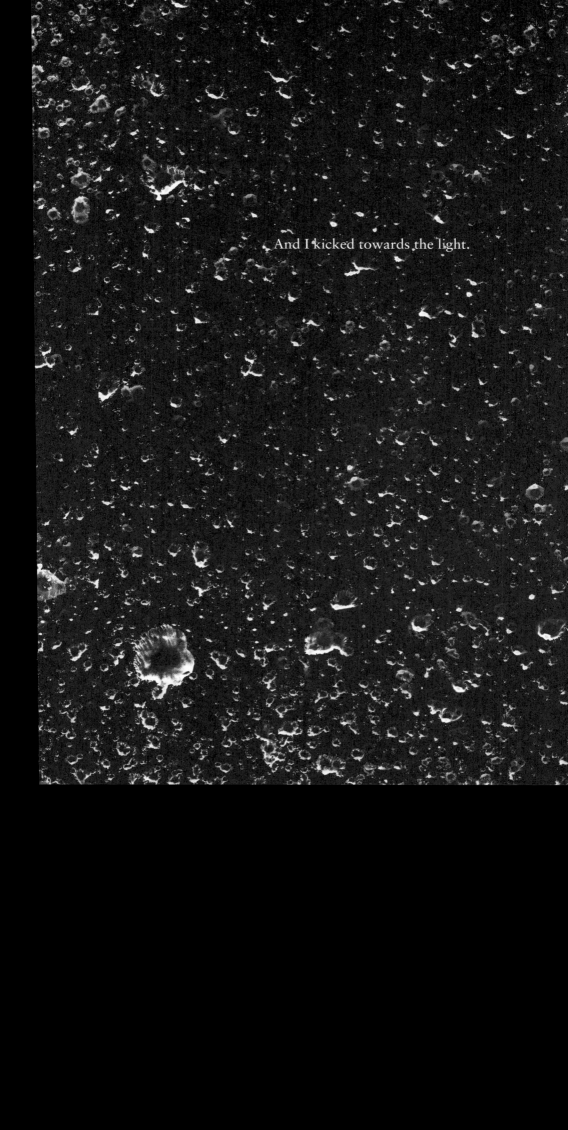

And I kicked towards the light.

Eighteen

I can't tell you for sure that a shark older than trees saved my life.
I can't tell you for sure that its enormous body moved beneath
me in a freezing sea and pushed me to the surface, where Captain
Bjorn and his boat were waiting.

But I can tell you that's what I believe, and doesn't that count
for something?

Captain Bjorn reached us just in time. He'd encountered Adrian
and Kin searching for me in town. Yes, you read that right. Adrian
and Kin together, looking for me. Weird, right? Weirder than me
being saved by a shark, I reckon.

They used Kin's telescope to search for me, and caught the

draglines, the froth coming from behind the boat. Captain Bjorn realized I was going after the shark alone, and he and his boat tailed me. He threw the life ring for me, and rescued Noodle from the boat.

I was unconscious and hypothermic, which means I was so cold from being in the sea I nearly died. I didn't, though, because Captain Bjorn knew just what to do. He tucked Noodle close to my heart, and she kept me warm while his crew rushed me to land. An air ambulance flew me to the hospital, the same one Mum got taken to. *Julia & the Shark* drifted almost to the Arctic, and Dad has had to pay a lot of money to get it retrieved.

He told me this once he had stopped crying long enough to speak. He and Mum were with me the whole time I was asleep. Mum had to get special permission because she is an inpatient at the psychiatric ward there. The ward is painted pale yellow, the color of an egg yolk from sad hens, and smells of antiseptic. It smells worse than the shark, but it's the safest place for her at the moment.

She told me the name for what she has, for what Grandma Julia had. Bipolar disorder, but it has nothing to do with the north and south poles—I checked. It means, like Dad explained, she swings between being really happy, and really sad. The happiness is as dangerous as the sadness. That's why she believed she could find the shark without any funding, without any help.

The sadness is so bad it means she can't feel anything happy and everything is hard, like moving through mud. She had an episode—that's what it's called when she feels really hyper or really low—before, after Grandma Julia died, while she was pregnant with me. This is what the **Never Again** meant on the back of that photo, Dad said. She never wanted to feel like that again. It wasn't to do with me at all. I still have to tell myself that, over and over. It wasn't my fault.

The first time I saw Mum after I found the shark, I was very tired, so I went to sleep again very fast, but when I surfaced again she was still there. She was dressed in one of her big cardigans, and the only thing that showed she was a patient was the bracelet on her wrist: 93875400.

"I heard," she said, "you've had an adventure."

"I suppose," I said. "I found the shark."

She brushed my hair back from my face, and kissed the top of my head.

"I did, didn't I?" I tried to sit up, but Mum soothed me gently. "I tagged it."

"They couldn't track it," said Dad gently.

"But I used the harpoon—" I looked at Mum desperately. "I saw it! I . . ."

I didn't want to tell her about the nudge at my legs, the way I felt like I was pushed towards the surface.

"I believe you," said Mum.

"I found it," I said again.

"I know," said Mum. "You were brilliant and clever and stupid. Julia, you could have . . . we might have . . ." She pulled me in closer. "You mustn't do things like that."

"Like what?"

"Dangerous things. Like going out on the boat on your own, especially in a storm."

"You did."

I felt her stiffen beside me, and Dad stared intently at her.

"Yes," said Mum slowly. "But I was sick. I am sick, J. My moods, they go up and down, up and down."

"Like waves."

"Exactly."

I swallowed, a new worry springing up like a jack-in-the-box. "Am I . . . will I be . . ."

"Like me?" Mum reached out and squeezed my hand. "No, Julia. There's plenty of your dad in there, too." I wrinkled my nose, and she laughed. "No two brains are the same. But if you ever feel strange, you tell me. You mustn't worry about that, J. We'll make sure you're always safe."

Before, I'd probably have been disappointed to not be exactly like Mum, but now I was glad Dad liked numbers and certainty and solidity. It meant the ground beneath my feet was stable, even if I loved being at sea.

"What was it like?"

"When I was doing all that, with the boat and the storms?" I nodded, and Mum sighed. "Honestly, I felt like I was invincible. Immortal. But it was silly, because I'm not. I needed to be more careful. And then, after the highest highs, I got low. I sank." She took hold of my hand. "But that's not going to happen again. I know the signs now, I'll be careful not to take on so much again. And they're going to give me medicine to help."

"You'll get better," I said firmly. "You can do anything."

"For you," said Mum. "I will."

"And yourself, Maura," said Dad. "We need to keep you on an even keel."

"Like *Julia & the Shark*." I grinned. "Where did it end up?"

"Reminds me," muttered Dad. "I need to check on it."

He went outside with his cell phone, because there's signal on Mainland, to call Captain Bjorn. Mum slid her hand into mine.

"We're going to donate it to Kin's family. They're going to use it as a library, moored in the harbor."

"Don't you need it? Now we know the shark's around—"

"Julia," she said, and her voice was thick. "I'm not going to look for the shark anymore."

I gaped at her. "But your research—"

"I love my work. I love you, too. And I love being well. And at the moment, I need to choose. And I choose to get better."

"Does this mean you're not a marine biologist anymore?"

"Silly." She poked me gently. "I'll always be a marine biologist. Just like I'll always be your mum, or always love Dad and Noodle. There are so many uncertainties in the world, but those are the things I'm sure of."

I threw myself forwards and hugged her. I believed her, just like she believed me. She would be better soon.

"I might need some time," she said, speaking into my hair, "in the hospital. When we get back to Cornwall."

Even though I wanted her home, wanted her dancing around the kitchen and making stupid jokes in the mornings, I knew she wouldn't ask unless she had no choice.

I squeezed her hand. "That's all right."

I realized then what I'd really found by finding the shark.

Remember at the beginning of this story, how I said I lost my mum? Really, what I meant was I lost my idea of Mum. The idea she was perfect and invincible and always right. But as well as the shark, I found the real Mum, with her complications and tangles and tears, and I love her just as much as ever. More, maybe. I told you to watch out for words, they are tricksy.

I also said what I was trying to get to was Mum. But now, I think that was a mistake. I think by spending all this time worrying about her, and caring about the things she cared about, I was losing myself. Mum and me aren't the same person, and that's all right.

Dad poked his head around the door.

"You have a visitor."

I knew who it would be, even without asking.

Dad stood aside, and Kin shuffled past him. He was looking at me through his bangs, his lips a tight line. He looked as nervous as I felt, and knowing that, seeing him, broke my fear like an egg. I nodded my best Neeta nod, and his face lit up. I know it's a cliché when people say that, but it's true. Like the lighthouse, he actually *beamed*.

Mum left us, and it was like that night with Adrian never happened. He told me about their search for me, and I told him about the shark, and an hour gulped by in a moment. Just before he had to leave, he pulled out a notebook from his coat pocket. It was nothing like my yellow one, lost in the sea. It was navy blue, with a gold *J* pressed into the front.

"I thought you'd want a new one of these."

I took hold of the notebook and opened it to a clean page. This wouldn't only be for sea creature facts. This would be for myths about stars and mountains and forests, and maybe a few numbers if Dad wanted. But first, Kin could tell me the names of the constellations.

I had found the impossible shark, but it hadn't been the answer Mum was looking for. Only she could find that, inside herself, by herself. It wasn't up to me to fix anything, to fix her.

Now I was ready to find something of my own. Something mine. Something new.

Nineteen

It's February, and the ground is cracking with frost. We've driven eight hours from Cornwall to reach Gretna Green, but that's nothing compared to Kin. His parents drove him here, and it took nearly a day and a half. Even though Unst is in the same country as Gretna Green, it's still a world away.

We had to time it perfectly, and we did. When we arrive, Kin and his parents are waiting in the parking lot. Even Neeta is here, and this time she actually smiles at me. I still do my cool nod back.

Dusk is gathering in the eaves of the trees above us, and Dad ensures I have my sweater and my coat on before he lets me run and hug Kin. He makes me wear extra layers all the time since I had hypothermia.

Once we've all said our hellos, Mum leads us away from the other people heading to the trail, and makes her own path through the trees, up a short hill where no one else is around. Dad grumbles about rule-breaking, but Mum only laughs. She's back to herself now, silly and giddy and working, but not so much we need to worry. I watch for the waves, the rough waters that carried her off last time, but she seems to have found her feet.

Kin's dad sets up his mended telescope, and we sit on the crest of the hill overlooking power lines, and wait. The sky is purple and deep-sea blue, melting into the dark ground. We wait a long time, and Dad frets, but Mum shushes him, tells him to be patient.

Kin and I sit a little way off. He tells me the floating library is a great success. "It's still called *Julia & the Shark*, but it's full of shelves now."

We talk about school, and how Adrian's getting on, about everything and nothing, even though we speak most weekends since I moved back to Cornwall. It's not the same as seeing him. It was easy to slip back into hanging out with Shabs and Nell and Matty, but none of them understand me like Kin. We're two whales on our own wavelength.

"Here," I say, and from my coat I take a piece of string. A rakhi, to show how we are more than just friends now, even though I'm back in Cornwall. To show we're family. I made it myself, tying blue and silver around each other, for the sea and the stars, which brought us together. "To say thanks for the notebook."

I tie it on his bony wrist, and we grin stupidly.

"Look, J, Kin!" Mum is calling and pointing, her camera ready.

It starts as a smudge, a gathering in the distance. It could almost be a wisp of cloud, but it moves like water. I say "it," but really, it's lots of things. Starlings, moving together, coming home to roost in the fields. A murmuration, just like Mum used to watch with Grandma Julia.

More and more gather, bunching and turning, like shoals of fish. Kin is watching through his dad's telescope, but I want to see it all, the whole picture, the birds darting and weaving as though patching invisible holes in the sky.

It's like they're being conducted,

    have practiced this a thousand times,

  and I know I'm gasping aloud and that Neeta can hear

      but I don't care. Cold is biting my ears,

and the rushing, tweeting sound of the starlings is enormous,

    like walking through a windswept forest in full leaf,

      or plunging

        into a freezing ocean.

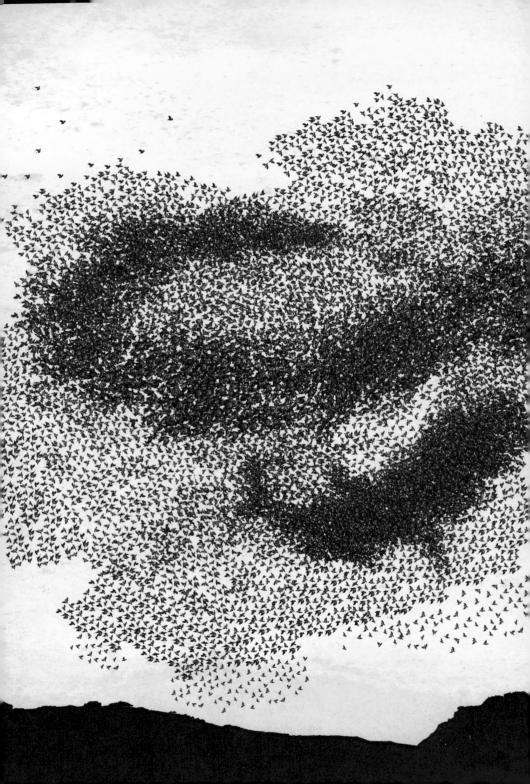

Mum takes my hand as the birds shimmer like a scarf,
lifting and lowering, like waves.
Until, finally, they find a safe place to land.

ACKNOWLEDGMENTS

Of all the stories we've told, this has the most of our hearts—and so it also has plenty of what others have given us. The love, the support, the belief, and the encouragement.

Our families are our pole stars, and this book is because of them: parents, siblings, grandparents, niblings, aunts, and uncles. Our especial thanks to Tilly, for modeling Julia, and to Andrea, for reading multiple drafts. Thank you to Tilly, Fred, Emily, Pippa, Isla, Ted, Leo, Albie, and Sabine, for inspiring us daily with your sheer existence.

We have been lucky to work with three extraordinary editors. Helen Thomas, who believed in and shaped Julia's story from the start, and ensured we remembered that "there's a crack in everything, that's how the light gets in." Sarah Lambert, who looked after us so beautifully and always showed such care and kindness. And to Rachel Wade, launching this book into the world. We're so excited for future adventures with you.

There are really three makers of this story. Alison Padley, our designer, has worked a deep and special enchantment on our words and images. You're a stone-cold genius.

Our team at Hachette Children's Group—it's a true delight to work with you. We feel part of a family and more than that, part of the magic you're weaving in the world of books. Special thanks to wonderful editor Nazima Abdillahi, our phenomenal publicist Emily Thomas, brilliant marketing director Naomi Berwin, amazing production controller Helen Hughes, and all the numerous people at HCG, Orion, and beyond, who willed and worked this book into existence.

Hellie Ogden—there are never the right words. Thank you for helping us through this next chapter, and finding us a safe place to land. Thank you to Rebecca Carter for looking after us, and all at Janklow & Nesbit UK. Thanks to Harriet Moore and all at David Higham Associates.

Thank you to Peter Mallet, photographer extraordinaire, who ensured nothing was lost in translation from paper artwork to digital files. Thank you to the broader network built around Tom's artwork: Paul Smith, Matt Price, Mandy Fowler, Freya Pocklington, Simon Palfrey, Pablo de Orellana, Mark Jones, and Ali Souleman.

Julia has had amazing cheerleaders from the very first moment. Thank you to some of our favorite authors and people: Katie Webber and Kevin Tsang, Kate Rundell, Cressida Cowell, Sophie Anderson, Ross Montgomery, Cat Doyle, Anna James, Florentyna Martin, Hilary McKay, Emma Carroll, and Tom Fletcher for their early, early support of this book.

Thank you to all at our lovely publishers over the pond, Union Square Kids. To our wonderful editor Laura Schreiber, Stefanie Chin, brilliant cover designer Marcie Lawrence, Whitney Manger, and everyone bringing Julia to readers across the States.

The children's, YA, and adult book community have been glorious champions of us and our work, as well as huge inspirations. Thank you especially to Lizzie Huxley-Jones, Anna James, Maz Evans, MG Leonard, Lucy Strange, Cat Doyle, Jasbinder Bilan, Sita Bramachari, James Nicols, Lauren James, Melinda Salisbury, Robin Stevens, Frances Hardinge, Mariam Khan, Aisha Bushby, Liz Hyder, Jessie Burton, Nikesh Shukla, Patrice Lawrence, Cat Johnson, and Samantha Shannon. Thank you to the Skunk Pirates for a safe space to speak all things writing.

Thank you to the booksellers from independent bookshops, including but not limited to Liznojan Books, the Kenilworth

Bookshop, The Book House, Mostly Books, Lighthouse Books, Portobello Books, Mainstreet Trading, Toppings St Andrews, and the bound. Thank you to the incredible teams at Waterstones, Blackwell's, and Foyles—especially our local Waterstones Oxford, and Oxford's two wonderful Blackwell's branches. We'd be lost without your support.

Librarians and teachers are the beating heart of the children's book community, and we are so thankful for how you champion stories as the truly life-changing things they are. We know there are so many of you in classrooms and libraries all over the country working to create a love of reading—you are the too-often unsung heroes of our industry. Special mention to Steph Elliot, who has been there since the beginning.

Thank you to all the bloggers and reviewers who spread the word about stories, so often for the sheer love of them. Special thanks to Fiona Noble, Simon Savidge, Gavin Hetherington, Jo Clarke, and Daniel Bassett.

Our beloved Daisy Johnson and Sarvat Hasin—stupid words. They are never enough. But we love you, we love your work, we love that we get to have you in our lives. Thank you for being there through the good, the bad, and the downright ugly.

To our wider community of friends. Each of you is so precious to us. Special thanks to those who were there while we wrestled with this story: Matt Bradshaw, Lucy Ayrton, Paul Fitchett, Laura Theis, Jess Oliver, and Elizabeth Macneal.

To four very loved children, whom we adore: Evie, Mira, Rowan, and TC.

To the various cats who have graced our laptops during the creation of this story—Luna, Oscar, and of course Noodle.

Thank you to you, the reader. Julia was ours, and now she's yours too.

To our twins, Rosemary and Lavender, who we hoped would one day hear this story. To our daughter, who will.

To each other, for it all.

FURTHER READING

See booktrust.org.uk/booklists for brilliant recommendations by theme. Here are some of our favorite books on these topics.

NATURE

The Lost Words—Robert Macfarlane and Jackie Morris (5+)

Beetle Boy trilogy—M.G. Leonard (8+)

A Wolf Called Wander—Rosanne Parry (8+)

Here We Are—Oliver Jeffers (3+)

Diary of a Young Naturalist—Dara McAnulty (12+)

MENTAL HEALTH

Paper Avalanche—Lisa Williamson (12+)

Tiny Infinities—J.H. Diehl (9+)

Am I Normal Yet?—Holly Bourne (14+)

Aubrey and the Terrible Yoot—Horatio Clare and Jane Matthews (8+)

The Red Tree—Shaun Tan (9+)

RESOURCES

The Greenland Shark is an extreme example of how amazing and bizarre nature can be. We believe protecting and conserving the natural world, both on land and in the sea, is of vital importance to all of us, because it impacts processes like climate change. But you don't have to live by the sea or be a marine biologist to help protect animals. Here are some resources where you can learn more about the natural world, and how to look after it.

nwf.org/Kids-and-Family—Fun family activities, contests, and ideas on how to connect with the outdoors

amnh.org/explore/ology/astronomy/a-kids-guide-to-stargazing—Kid-friendly stargazing guide, sky journal, and interactive star map from the American Museum of Natural History

nature-shetland.co.uk—Amazing pictures and stories about wildlife in Shetland

marine-conservation.org/mpatlas—Interactive maps that simulate conservation efforts and at-risk areas

worldwildlife.org/teaching-resources—The WWF is the world's leading conservation organization

Julia's mum has a mental illness called bipolar disorder. As you have read, it can be easily managed with the right support. There's a whole range of mental health issues, and not all of them are as severe as what Julia's mum experiences. But sometimes we all feel a bit sad or overwhelmed, and might not know how to deal with it. We believe it's so important to talk about these feelings without shame or embarrassment, because that's the only way to process them. Both of us, Kiran and Tom, have experienced this ourselves.

The most important thing is getting the right support, and the only way to do that is to talk to a trusted adult—a parent, a teacher, a school counselor, or use one of the resources below to speak to a trained professional. The more we talk, the less we bottle up, and the better we feel. Here are some places you can learn more about the issues we talk about in *Julia and the Shark*.

teenline.org—Online support group run by teens, for teens

erikaslighthouse.org/teens—Extensive resources for educating and acting on mental health issues in the classroom and at home

kidshealth.org/en/kids—For anyone wanting to learn more about their mental health and how to protect it

nimh.nih.gov/get-involved—National Institute of Mental Health has guides on all kinds of mental health struggles, including kids' mental health—just click on the "Digital Shareables" tab

ymhproject.org/resources—The Youth Mental Health Project has different hotlines for your needs, as well as a wealth of resources for kids and parents, including those specific to racism and COVID-19

thetrevorproject.org/resources/category/mental-health—Mental health resources specifically for LGBTQ+ teens

nipinthebud.org—Informative and approachable videos to get kids talking about mental health

crisistextline.org—Text "START" to 741741 to message with a trained professional about how you're feeling

ABOUT THE AUTHORS

Kiran Millwood Hargrave and Tom de Freston met in 2009, when Kiran was a student and Tom was artist-in-residence at Cambridge University. They have been a couple and collaborators ever since, but *Julia and the Shark* is their first novel. Kiran is the award-winning, bestselling author of stories including *The Girl of Ink & Stars*, *The Way Past Winter*, and *The Deathless Girls*, and Tom is making his illustration debut, having worked as an acclaimed artist for many years.

HOUGHTON MIFFLIN
Reading
A Legacy of Literacy

Nature's Fury

HOUGHTON MIFFLIN

BOSTON • MORRIS PLAINS, NJ

California • Colorado • Georgia • Illinois • New Jersey • Texas

Design, Art Management and Page Production: Kirchoff/Wohlberg, Inc.

ILLUSTRATION CREDITS
4-25 Karen Chandler. **27-29, 31, 33-42, 44-47** Todd Leonardo. **52-53, 55-56, 63** Mike DiGiorgio.

PHOTOGRAPHY CREDITS
26 (bkgd) PhotoDisc. **26** (i) Corbis. **27** PhotoDisc. **28** Karl Weatherly/ Corbis. **30** Galen Russell/Corbis. **32** Chris Rainer/Corbis. **36** AP/Wide World Photos. **43** Superstock. **45** AFP/Corbis. **47** PhotoDisc. **48** (bkgd) PhotoDisc. **48** (i) Mike Magnuson/Tony Stone Images. **49** The Granger Collection, New York. **50** Corbis/Bettmann. **51** AP/Wide World Photos. **52** Gregory G. Dimijian/Photo Researchers. **53** Richard Hamilton Smith/ Corbis. **54** Lester Lefkowitz/The Stock Market. **55** Larry Mayer/Liaison International. **57** Jeff Christensen/Liaison International. **58** (t) Gregory Foster/Liaison International. **58** (b) Liaison International. **59** Larry Mayer/ Liaison International. **60** The Granger Collection, New York. **61** The Granger Collection, New York. **62** (t) Jose Pelaez/The Stock Market. **62** (b) Swedberg/Bruce Coleman, Inc. **63** AP/Wide World Photos. **64** AP/ Wide World Photos. **65** Lewis/Liaison International. **66** Lewis/Liaison International. **67** Wernher Krutein/Liaison International. **68** PhotoDisc. **69** (t) PhotoDisc. **69** (b) Mike Magnuson/Tony Stone Images.

Printed in U.S.A.

ISBN: 0-618-04406-X

9-VH-05 04 03

Nature's Fury

Contents

▶ **Riding Out the Storm** **4**
by Kathryn Snyder
illustrated by Karen Chandler

▶ **White Dragon: Anna Allen in the
Face of Danger.** **26**
by Maryann Dobeck
illustrated by Todd Leonardo

▶ **Floods** **48**
by Barbara Brooks Simons
illustrated by Mike DiGiorgio

Riding Out the Storm

by Kathryn Snyder
illustrated by Karen Chandler

Strategy Focus

Raylee is home alone, and a hurricane is on the way! Will she be able to ride out the storm? As you read, try to **predict** what will happen next.

Where's Aunt Luelle?

Raylee looked out the window. The sky was gray and ashy. It looked the color of the Gulf of Mexico waters. Raylee could see huge waves in the distance. It sure looked like a storm was coming.

Raylee's parents had taped the windows last night. They hadn't thought the wooden shutters were needed. But the storm watch of last night had become a hurricane warning in the past two hours. People who lived in low-lying areas were heading for the shelters. That's just what Raylee was going to do — head for the shelter. She'd go the minute that Aunt Luelle came by.

Momma had called from work around ten and told Raylee, "I'll try to pick you up at noon. If I can't do it, Aunt Luelle will. She'll be by at one o'clock. We'll meet at the shelter. We have plenty of time. The storm won't really hit until later this afternoon."

Well, Momma hadn't come at noon. It was nearly one. Drops of rain splattered against the window, leaving spots the size of quarters. *Where are you, Aunt Luelle?* Raylee thought. *Chomper and I are waiting.* Raylee suddenly froze. Where was that dog?

Storms always upset Chomper. "Chomper!" Raylee called. "Chomper. Come here! *Now!*" There was no sign of the dog.

Raylee walked through the house. She looked under beds and in closets. Then, glancing out the kitchen window, she saw Chomper by the fence. "Come back, right now!" Raylee yelled. Chomper wouldn't come.

Raylee dashed out into the rain. Chomper darted around the corner. He disappeared into the next yard. Raylee fought through the wind, looking for her lost mutt. She finally spotted him under the neighbor's porch.

It took Raylee nearly twenty minutes to get him out.
At one point, Raylee thought she heard a car horn. But
the wind made things sound strange. So, she didn't
think it was Aunt Luelle. Finally she got Chomper to
crawl close enough that she could grab his collar.

Raylee dragged Chomper back into the house just
in time to see Aunt Luelle drive off. "No!" she screamed.
She ran outside and waved at the car. But Aunt Luelle
didn't see her. *She must have thought I went with Momma,*
Raylee realized.

Storm Power

Raylee slammed the door behind her. "Bad dog!" she yelled at Chomper. Then Raylee knelt to hug him. "I know," Raylee said gently. "You were just scared." Saying the word *scared* sent a chill up Raylee's neck. What would she do now?

Raylee changed into dry clothes. Then she turned on the TV in the kitchen. The news showed people in a shelter. She wondered if she'd see Momma or Aunt Luelle.

When she turned to fill a plastic bottle with water, Raylee heard a noise. SNAP! The TV screen went gray. The refrigerator stopped humming too.

The power was out. Raylee grabbed the phone. But when she punched in 9-1-1, there was silence. The phone was dead too.

The kitchen window streamed with water. Through it, Raylee could see trees bending helplessly in the wind. The storm was starting to get much worse.

Well, Raylee decided, *I'll just have to ride the storm out*. That's what Aunt Luelle always said — *ride the storm out*. It meant making do until the storm was over — all by herself.

Aunt Luelle never forgot riding out Hurricane Carla back in 1961. She said it was the scariest experience of her life. She also said she'd make sure no family member ever rode out another hurricane. *But hadn't Aunt Luelle just driven off and left me to ride this storm out alone?* Raylee thought.

The wind shrieked like a wild animal. Water poured over the sides of the roof. Raylee sat on a chair in the living room. She had a flashlight and a bottle of water with her. Chomper lay at her feet. He lifted his head now and then to cry.

The pictures shook on the walls.

Water and Wind

Raylee squinted to see through the window. The street had turned into a river. The driveway was like a lake. Water was roaring against the front door.

Raylee walked away from the window. Suddenly, the wind blew it out with a BOOM.

Chomper howled. Raylee grabbed his collar and led him into the bathroom. The bathroom was the safest place to be. Its pipes were fixed to the earth. Raylee sat under the sink and and held Chomper. The wind whistled through the plumbing. WHOOOO! WHOOOO!

Then came horrible noises of the front door cracking apart. Water was pouring into the house! It was coming into the bathroom!

15

Raylee jumped up. The water was at her ankles, then her knees. It was rising higher!

She pushed out of the bathroom into the hallway. Chairs and tables floated and crashed everywhere.

With a mighty jump, Raylee reached the handle to the attic door. She used every bit of strength to pull the door down. She ran up the stairs and called to Chomper to follow.

The two of them sat at the edge of the attic opening. Below them was a dark, noisy, dirty river of water. Raylee flashed her flashlight over the surface. She thought she saw a dead fish.

The attic was tiny. But at least it was dry — for now. But Raylee knew that an attic was exactly the wrong place to be during a hurricane.

Aunt Luelle had told her how in 1961 a neighbor's roof had blown right off.

Please, roof, stay put, Raylee thought.

Riding It Out

Raylee sat, leaning against the wall. Chomper sat right beside her. The rain sounded like a thousand drummers. It beat above their heads for hours.

Then suddenly it was quiet. *The eye of the storm,* Raylee thought. She knew that was the middle of the storm, where everything was calm. But it would only be quiet for a short time.

Raylee could see the late afternoon sunlight on the water below. The water was now halfway up the hallway walls. She could go down there and swim. But the water looked so dirty. There were probably snakes in it too. Raylee decided to stay where she was.

Soon the quiet ended. The wind blew wildly against the roof again. Except for the flashlight's light, everything was dark now. A square metal roof vent clattered under the pounding rain.

The roof shook harder, harder, and even harder. Raylee prayed that the wind would not lift the roof, her, and Chomper into the dark sky.

Through the Roof!

Hour after hour, Raylee and Chomper waited. Would the winds never die down? The flashlight ran out. All Raylee could do was sit in the dark and wait. Every so often, she would fall asleep.

Towards morning, something woke Raylee from one of her cat naps. It was the sound of a helicopter right above the house. Rescue! But how could Raylee let the rescuers know where she was?

Raylee looked above her. The early morning light was coming through the metal roof vent above her. She began to pull at it. She needed something hard to hit it with. All she had was the flashlight. It would have to work.

Raylee held the flashlight at one end. She pounded against the vent with all her might. The vent began to move. In just a few minutes, the vent was off.

Raylee pounded at the wood and shingles. Soon the hole was big enough for Raylee to push her head and shoulders through. A gentle rain was now falling.

"Here! Here!" she yelled.

The people in the helicopter saw her! The helicopter headed toward her. She waved her hands over her head.

Before long, a rescuer was being lowered from the helicopter. Soon Raylee and Chomper would be safe.

She had made it through a hurricane — all alone. She had been able to ride out the storm.

Responding

Think About the Selection

1 What kind of storm hits Raylee's town?

2 What does "riding out a storm" mean?

3 What are the first three things that Raylee does after Aunt Luelle leaves?

Sequence of Events

Copy this chart on a piece of paper. Fill in the events. Then complete charts like this one for the other parts of the story.

Part of story: Where's Aunt Luelle?			
Event 1	**Event 2**	**Event 3**	**Event 4**
Raylee wakes up.	She talks to Momma on the phone.	?	?

25

White Dragon:

Anna Allen in the Face of Danger

by Maryann Dobeck

illustrations by Todd Leonardo

Strategy Focus

Anna Allen loved the snow. She never dreamed it would almost kill her. As you read, think of **questions** about the story that you want answered.

Mountains of Snow

In 1982, it snowed hard in the Sierra Nevada, a chain of mountains in California. By late March, the mountains lay beneath a deep cover of snow. Business was booming for the ski resorts there. All day long, skiers rode up the mountainsides and skied down the smooth white slopes.

Skiers fly down the slopes of Alpine Meadows, overlooking Lake Tahoe.

Anna Allen worked at the Alpine Meadows Ski Resort near Lake Tahoe. She ran the chair lift that takes skiers up the mountains so that they can ski down. It was a good job for a 22-year-old woman who loved the outdoors. She loved skiing. And every day, she could look at some of the most beautiful mountains in the world.

On the last day of March, Anna awoke to a fresh layer of snow. It was six feet deep in some places. Throughout the day, heavy wet snow continued to fall. Anna wanted to help a friend dig out his car from under the snow. She needed her waterproof ski pants. They were in a locker at the ski resort. Anna set off for the resort to get them.

When steep slopes can hold no more snow, the snow begins to slide. Some avalanches reach speeds of 200 miles per hour.

Blasting the Slopes

The mountain manager was in charge of making things safe for skiers at the resort. He had closed the resort that day. He knew that the heavy snow might slide down the slopes and become an avalanche. Without warning, tons of snow could come crashing down the mountainside. An avalanche could snap trees, smash buildings, and bury skiers.

The locker room was in a three-story building near the ski lodge. As Anna went into the building, she met the mountain manager. He seemed upset with her.

He told Anna that she had just done something foolish and dangerous. "You skied on the main road!" he pointed out. A team was getting ready to blast the snow on that road. Anna had just missed getting caught in the blasting.

Skilled blasters help prevent large avalanches.

Trained workers blast the slopes to make small avalanches. Setting off a few small avalanches can stop big avalanches from happening. Big avalanches can be deadly.

But getting caught in an area being blasted can be deadly too. Anna had not known about the blasting. She had been very lucky to miss it.

Buried Alive

Anna knew how lucky she had been. If she had known they were blasting the slopes, she never would have gone to the lodge. She hurried to the hall lined with lockers. She would just grab her ski pants and head home.

CRASH! Suddenly something hard hit her. Everything went black.

When Anna awoke, she had trouble thinking clearly. Her head hurt terribly. She looked around, but she didn't know where she was. At first she thought she was at home. She thought that maybe the hot water heater had blown up. Or maybe there had been an earthquake. Slowly her thoughts became clearer. "An avalanche," she realized.

Anna could feel the wooden lockers that had fallen against a bench to form a space. The space was only about three feet wide and five feet long. She could not see. It was as dark as night and as cold as a refrigerator. There was little room for her to move. Anna was not sure that she would leave this place alive.

Searchers Start Looking

A large avalanche had rushed down from the slopes above. It had smashed the building to pieces before coming to a stop in a nearby parking lot.

A lucky man at one end of the building was able to dig himself out. Searchers were already on the scene. How many other people might be buried in the building and under the snow?

Two searchers had seen Anna walk toward another part of the building. That part of the lodge looked completely destroyed. It didn't seem possible that anyone there could have survived. They would try looking there later. For now, searchers chose a different spot to hunt in.

Rescue workers and dogs search for people buried under the snow.

Bridget the Rescue Dog

Later the next day, the search moved back to the building where Anna was trapped. The searchers brought in specially trained rescue dogs. These dogs are trained to find buried people by sniffing the snow. Then they help the searchers dig the people out of the snow.

On the third day, a rescue dog named Bridget barked loudly. Someone was buried! Bridget stood over the spot where Anna lay trapped. Several searchers listened for someone below. But they couldn't hear anything.

It had begun to snow heavily again. The dogs and the rescue workers couldn't keep looking. For the time being, the search had to be called off.

Days Under Snow

While the people above looked for Anna, she fought for her life as best as she could. She had found some matches. Their light helped her find warm clothing in the lockers. It hurt to move her body, but she pulled on several layers. Still she shivered from the cold. Her teeth chattered. Could she stay warm enough for long enough?

In the darkness, Anna heard a dog barking. The sound came from above her. A rescue dog! Anna shouted and shouted. "I'm here! I'm down here!" But the dog's barking soon stopped. She heard the sounds of people moving away. In deep snow, sounds easily travel down, but not up. She realized that the rescuers must not have heard her.

Anna knew that another avalanche might happen at any time. Maybe that was why the searchers had moved away. "I would hate to have someone else die trying to find me," she thought.

Anna had nothing to eat but snow. She felt weak from hunger and cold. She worried that she might pass out before the searchers came again. If she fell asleep for too long, she could easily die. She fought to stay awake.

Search and Rescue

Snow fell heavily for two more days. Then the skies cleared. The searchers began their work again.

Bridget sniffed again at the spot above Anna. Again, she barked. Someone was down there. This time, the searchers stayed. They began digging. They dug deeper and deeper until they hit a board. They pulled the board away to find a hand reaching up through the snow.

"Anna, is that you?" the searchers yelled down.

"Of course it is!" she called back weakly.

Anna grabbed a searcher's hand. He pulled. She crawled up into daylight. It had taken five long, cold days, but now she was free!

A helicopter carrying Anna lifted off while the rescuers cheered.

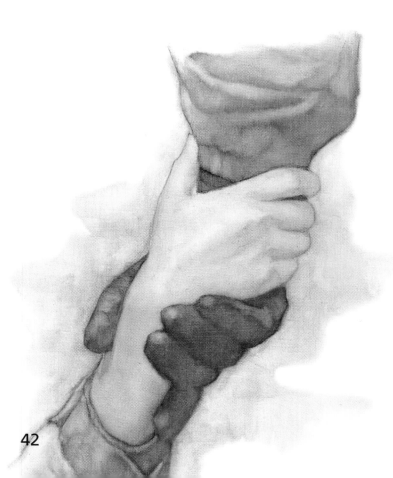

Back on the Slopes

At the hospital, Anna was in very bad shape. Her legs had been in the cold for too long. In the end, she lost her right leg below the knee and all the toes on her left foot.

Anna learned to walk with an artificial leg. She refused to feel sorry for herself. Within a year, she was back skiing. Nearly a year after the avalanche, she entered a race for disabled skiers. "I've got to keep going," she said.

The White Dragon

There is an old riddle that is told in snow country. It goes like this: *What flies without wings, hits without hands, and sees without eyes?* The answer is a *White Dragon*. It's another name for an avalanche.

People look over the damage done by a White Dragon.

Today Anna Allen works at the Mammoth Mountain Ski Resort in California. She visits schools and teaches ski safety. She tells of the five days in March 1982 when she was trapped by an avalanche. She hopes her story will help others know the fury of the White Dragon.

Responding

Think About the Selection

1. Why is the mountain manager upset with Anna?

2. Why don't the rescue workers hear Anna shouting the first time?

3. How do the headings help you read the story?

Using Headings

Make a chart like this on a piece of paper. For every heading in the story, write what that part of the story tells about.

Heading	This part of the story tells about...
Mountains of Snow	The Sierra Nevada mountains where Anna Allen works
Blasting the Slopes	?
Buried Alive	?
Searchers Start Looking	?
Bridget the Rescue Dog	?
Days Under Snow	?

FLOODS

by Barbara Brooks Simons

Strategy Focus

In this selection, you'll read about two types of floods. **Monitor** your reading to make sure you understand each type. Reread parts to **clarify** anything you don't understand.

Ancient Egyptians depended on the Nile River for food, travel, and water for crops.

People have lived near water throughout time. Being near a river or ocean can make life easier. Rivers give people water for drinking, swimming, and growing crops. Rivers and oceans give people food, such as fish and water birds. People also use rivers and oceans for boat travel.

But living near water can also be dangerous. The greatest danger comes from floods. In the United States, about 20 million people live in places where floods are likely.

Moving water can be very strong. Flood waters knock down trees and carry away houses. Towns can be lost. People and animals can drown.

Flood waters tipped this house and sent a tree through a second-floor window in Johnstown, PA in 1889.

A farm in Iowa is covered by flood waters in 1998.

Ocean floods are caused by very big storms or other unusual events, such as earthquakes. In the United States, river floods are much more common. Why do they happen? The easiest answer is, "Too much water."

River floods can happen at any time. They are more likely in late winter and early spring.   Heavy rain or melting snow can make streams or rivers overflow onto the land and cover fields and roads. Frozen ground can't soak up all the water.

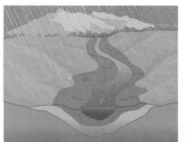

Left: Too much water from rain or snow can cause a river to overflow its banks.

Below: Rain causes high waters in this Louisiana swamp.

Left: Ice blocking a river causes water to overflow the river's banks.

Below: Ice covers the Mississippi River.

Ice is another problem. Sometimes ice blocks the water in a river. The water stops moving. Tons of water build up behind the ice, flooding the land upstream. When the ice melts, water moves downstream very quickly and causes more flooding.

The Hoover Dam was built on the Colorado River in the 1930s. It holds back enough water to cover the entire state of Pennsylvania with one foot of water!

Too much water can also make dams break. Dams are giant walls made to block water and control how it flows. They often hold back tons of water. When dams break, the flood is quick and deadly.

Today, people know how to build safe, strong dams. But not long ago, many dams were just piles of dirt. They were not very safe.

The Mississippi is the largest river in the United States. It moves through a wide valley down the center of the country. There have always been floods along the Mississippi. In many places, people have made walls of earth or concrete along the river's banks. These walls are called *levees*. Levees help block water from coming onto the land.

Above: The Mississippi River flood plain in Iowa is covered with flood water.

Right: The flat land on either side of a river is the flood plain.

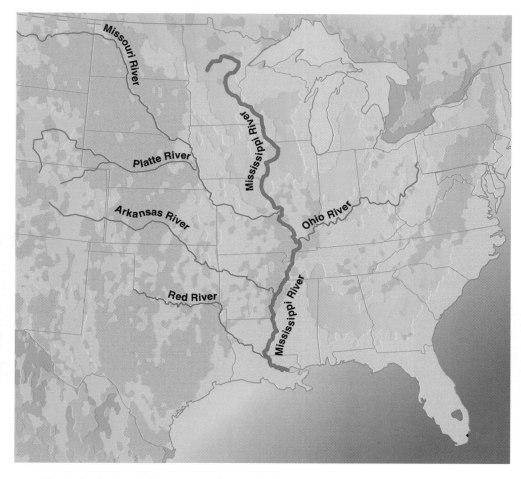

The Mississippi River runs through the center of the United States. A number of other big rivers flow into the Mississippi.

The Mississippi River gets its water from a large part of the United States. Hundreds of smaller rivers send water into the Mississippi.

A photographer guides a boat across Mississippi flood waters that covered this farm in 1993.

Some years are worse for floods than others. In the Midwest, people will not forget 1993. Winter snows and spring rain had soaked the ground. In June, more rain began. It fell week after week. The ground couldn't soak it up. So water began to move onto the land all along the Mississippi.

The levees could not hold back the water. People rushed to pile up bags of sand, but water moved over fields and washed into houses. The worst floods along the Mississippi were in Iowa, Missouri, and Illinois. From the air, Iowa looked like a huge lake. In all, the floods hit 12,000 square miles in nine states. About 70,000 people lost their homes. Fifty people lost their lives.

Missouri residents use sandbags to build up a levee in July, 1993.